VOLKSWAGEN BLUES

VOLKSWAGEN BLUES

JACQUES POULIN

TRANSLATED BY
SHEILA FISCHMAN

Cormorant Books

The publisher gratefully acknowledges the support of the
Canada Council for the Arts and the Ontario Arts Council
for its publishing program. We acknowledge the financial support
of the Government of Canada through the Book Publishing
Industry Development Program (BPIDP) for our publishing activities.

Second printing, November 2004
Printed and bound in Canada

National Library of Canada Cataloguing in Publication

Poulin, Jacques, 1937–
Volkswagen blues

Translation of: Volkswagen blues.
ISBN 1-896951-42-2

I. Fischman, Sheila II. Title.

PS8531.O82V6413 2002 C843'.54 C2002-900033-5
PQ3919.2.P59V6413 2002

English translation of an excerpt from "Le Bateau espagnol,"
by Leo Ferre, by Donald Winkler.

Cover design: Angel Guerra
Text design: Tannice Goddard
Cover image: Bildhuset AB/Photonica

CORMORANT BOOKS INC.
215 SPADINA AVENUE, STUDIO 230, TORONTO, ON CANADA M5T 2C7
www.cormorantbooks.com

This translation is dedicated
to the memory of John Goodwin

"We are no longer the heroes of history."

— EMMET GROGAN, *RINGOLEVIO*

I

Jacques Cartier

He was wakened by the meowing of a cat.

He sat up in his sleeping bag and drew aside the curtain that covered the back window of the Volkswagen minibus: he saw a tall thin girl in a white nightgown walking barefoot in the grass despite the cold; a black kitten was running behind her.

He tapped on the window, not too hard, and the kitten stopped dead, one paw in the air, then started running again. The girl's hair was as black as coal and plaited into a long braid that hung to the middle of her back.

The man craned his neck and saw that she was heading for the section of the campground that was reserved for tents. He got out of his sleeping bag, pulled on his jeans and a heavy woollen sweater because he was sensitive to the cold, then he opened all the curtains in the old Volks. The sun was rising, and there were patches of fog over the Baie de Gaspé.

He went to the restroom to wash and shave. When he came back there was no one in the tent area; the girl had disappeared. He opened the sliding door of the van and carried his portable gas stove, his tank of propane and his plastic dishes to the picnic table. He prepared orange juice, cornflakes and toast, and boiled enough water for coffee and the dishes. When he'd got to the coffee he rose abruptly from the table and went to get his brother Théo's old postcard from the glove compartment. He propped the card against the marmalade jar and slowly sipped his coffee.

When the man looked up, he saw that the fog had lifted and the Baie de Gaspé was flooded with light. He washed his dishes, then replaced everything in the minibus and slid back the roof.

Before he left, he made his customary three checks: the ice in the fridge, the motor oil, the fan belt. Everything was normal. Mechanically he gave the front tire on the driver's side a kick, then got behind the wheel. He drove out of the campground and turned left: the town of Gaspé was about five kilometres away.

The hill was fairly steep so he had to gear down to third, then to second, and when he reached the top he spotted the tall thin girl walking along the side of the road. She was partly concealed by a huge knapsack with a tubular frame, but he recognized her at once by her very black hair and her bare feet. He deliberately stayed in second longer than necessary, and when she heard the rumbling of the motor, the girl stuck out her left thumb without turning around. He drove past her, stopped the Volks on the shoulder and flashed his emergency lights.

The girl opened the door.

She had a bony face, a dark complexion and very black, slightly slanted eyes. She wore a white cotton dress.

"Bonjour!" she said.

"I'm going to Gaspé," said the man. "It's not very far, but . . ."

He waved her inside.

She shrugged off her knapsack and hoisted it onto the passenger seat. The black kitten emerged from one of the pockets and climbed up on the back of the seat. He was all black with short hair and blue eyes. He started to explore the van. The man wedged the knapsack between the two seats. The girl got inside, but she left the door of the Volks open. She watched the kitten and waited until he had finished his exploration. Eventually he came and lay in her lap.

"It's all right," she said, and shut the door.

The man glanced in the rearview mirror, then started up.

The Volks was very old and covered with rust, but the motor ran well. It was a rebuilt motor. The girl was young. The man adjusted the heat so she would get some warm air on her feet. It was early May.

"Are you going far?" he asked.

"I've no idea," she said. "First I have to go to the Gaspé museum. I know someone there I want to say hello to."

"I'm going to Gaspé myself, but I don't know where exactly . . ."

He gestured broadly with his right hand.

"I'm looking for my brother," he said at last.

He had not seen his brother for a very long time: fifteen years, maybe twenty — he couldn't remember exactly. The last time he'd seen him was at Mont-Tremblant, where they had watched a car race. Formula Ones. Then his brother had gone on a trip. At first he had sent postcards. He must have been moving around a lot because the cards had come from all sorts of places; one was from Key West, another from James Bay. Then, some years later, he had stopped writing. There had been no word from him. The last postcard was very peculiar and the stamp had been canceled at Gaspé.

"Look in the glove compartment," he said.

The girl took out the postcard and examined it closely. The man watched out of the corner of his eye to see her reaction. The card showed a typical Gaspé landscape: a small fishing village in the hollow of a cove; the message on the back was totally illegible except for the signature: *"Your brother Théo."*

Camille Pouliot, *La grande aventure de Jacques Cartier*, p. 42.

"Obviously it's old handwriting," said the girl.

"Obviously," said the man, holding his breath.

"Old texts are always hard to read," she said very calmly. "Is your brother Théo a historian or something like that?"

"He studied history, but he's never worked in the field. Or any other field. He didn't like to work. What he liked was trips and cars. He'd do odd jobs and when he got a bit of money he'd travel."

The girl smiled faintly.

"And what did he look like?"

"The opposite of me: tall, almost six feet, and his hair was . . . black, like yours, and he wouldn't work himself into a state over nothing."

"But, if you don't mind my asking, why are you looking for him *now*? After all, the postcard's very old."

"That's true. I stuck it in a book and forgot it. I mean, I couldn't remember what book it was in."

He thought for a moment.

"Of course that doesn't answer your question."

"You don't have to."

"I know."

The man was driving the Volks very slowly, in third gear. From time to time he looked in the rearview mirror to see if anyone behind him was getting impatient. Then eventually he stopped by the side of the road and switched off the ignition.

"I turned forty last week and . . ."

He shook his head.

"Actually it has nothing to do with age . . . Some days you feel as if everything's falling apart . . . inside you and all around you," he said, searching for the right words. "So then you try to figure out what you can hang on to . . . I thought of my brother. He used to be my best friend. I wondered why I'd stopped hearing from him, and I looked for the last card he'd sent me. And finally I found it. It was in a book with a gold cover called *The Golden Dream*. By Walker Chapman. Have you read it?"

"No," said the girl.

"Anyway, that's where I found the card. And since it had been mailed in Gaspé, even though it was a long time ago . . ."

"I understand."

"Today I feel old and ridiculous."

The girl resumed her scrutiny of the postcard. She absent-mindedly stroked the head of the kitten, who was asleep in her lap.

"Is your name Jack?" she asked, reading the name and address to the right of the message.

"That's what my brother used to call me. When we were little we gave ourselves English names; we thought they suited us much better!"

"People call me La Grande Sauterelle. They say it's because my legs are way too long, like a grasshopper's."

She pulled her dress up to her thighs to show him. Her legs really were very long and very thin. Then she turned to the post-card again.

"The last word looks as if it might be *cross*," she said.

She handed him the card.

"You may be right," he said, "but couldn't it be *loss*?"

"No."

"Why not?"

"Because it has five letters."

He started to laugh and she looked at him, uncomprehending.

"I'm sorry," he said, "but I think we look like a couple of *zouaves* trying to decipher some old buried treasure map!"

"We are, in a way," she said, her manner still serious. "If your brother has taken the trouble to have an old text printed on a postcard, there must have been a reason. He was sending a message, don't you think?"

She spoke calmly, and it was very pleasant to hear her thinking out loud.

"Unless it's a joke," she added.

"It's hard to know," he said. "Théo didn't do things like other people."

He switched on the motor again.

"If I were you," said the girl, "I'd go to the museum and show this card to the curator."

He turned around to look at her. She still had the same grave, thoughtful expression, but her head was bent to one side because the kitten had climbed up on her shoulder and settled against her neck.

"HERE WE ARE," said La Grande Sauterelle. "Turn left."

Jack turned off the road and parked the old Volks beside the museum. It was a frame structure with several sections arranged in a star. Beyond it, on a sort of platform, stood a group of black metal sculptures that resembled menhirs and bore inscriptions; there was also a tall granite cross that stood at least nine metres high.

They got out of the Volks. The girl left her cat inside, but she opened a window so he could go outside if he wanted.

"Won't he get lost?" the man worried.

"No," she said. "He likes to walk around, but he never goes far."

In the museum lobby an old woman was washing the floor with a mop and a bucket of water. The young girl approached her and spoke to her in a low voice. Jack walked around the soapy puddles and headed for the information counter, behind which was seated a young man who seemed absorbed in a book.

"Sorry to bother you."

"Huh?" said the young man, looking up.

"I'd like some information, please."

"What kind of information?"

"About this," said Jack, showing him the postcard.

The young man peered at the text for a moment, glanced at the other side of the card, then looked again at the text.

"I don't understand a word," he declared.

"I know, but . . ."

"If you already knew, why did you show me the card?" the young man interrupted impatiently.

"It's old writing."

"So what?"

Just then La Grande Sauterelle and the cleaning woman came over to the counter. Without raising his voice, the man tried to explain: "I wanted to ask for information about the source of the text . . ."

"I'm not an expert on old texts," said the young man curtly.

He handed back the postcard with a shrug and returned to his reading. It was a *Superman* comic.

La Grande Sauterelle asked, "Do you know if the curator's in his office?"

"Who?" asked the young man without looking up.

"The director of the museum."

"He's away."

The cleaning woman tried to look at the card over Jack's shoulder. She was short and plump, and the colour of her skin, as well as her features, showed that she was an Indian.

"May I look?" she asked.

He said nothing, so she wiped her fingers on her white smock and took the card from his hands.

"It looks to me exactly like Jacques Cartier's handwriting," she said.

There was a long moment's silence. When she realized that no one had anything to say, the woman laid the postcard on the counter and returned to the bucket of water she had left in the middle of the lobby.

"Jacques Cartier's handwriting? Why do you say that?" asked the man, who had followed her step by step.

"It's simple," she said. "Your old text is exactly the same as the one in the main hall, and I couldn't be wrong about it because every day when I do the cleaning I have to dust the two placards."

"*Two* placards? So there are *two* texts?"

"Not at all. It's the same text on both placards, except that on one it's written in old writing like yours and on the other in . . . ordinary writing."

"Would you be so kind as to show us?" he asked briskly.

"Certainly. Come this way, but watch your step."

Jack and the girl followed the cleaning woman into the main hall. They walked along a sort of corridor marked off by parallel cables that snaked past a variety of objects that were scattered on the floor, hung on the wall or exhibited in glass cases: tools, articles of clothing, weapons, transport vehicles, navigational instruments, cards and posters, all arranged in chronological order, from the early days of America to the present time.

At the back of the main hall the cleaning woman stopped in front of two huge posters. She took a cloth from her pocket and automatically dusted them.

"Here it is," she said straightforwardly. They saw at once that the text on the poster on the left was the same as that on the postcard, and they immediately turned to thank the woman, but she had already gone.

The right-hand poster read: "Excerpt from the original account of Jacques Cartier's first voyage." And the text, in block letters, was as follows:

> On the twenty-fourth day of the said month, we had a cross made thirty feet high, which was put together in the presence of a number of the Indians on the point at the entrance to this harbour, under the cross-bar of which we fixed a shield with three fleur-de-lys in relief, and above it a wooden board, engraved in large Gothic characters, where was written long live the King of France. We erected this cross on the point in their presence and they watched it being put together and set up. And when it had been raised in the air, we all knelt down with our hands joined, worshipping it before them; and made signs to them, looking up and pointing towards heaven, that by means of this we had our redemption, at which they showed many marks of admiration, at the same time turning and looking at the cross.

"It's a fine text and I'm glad to have read it," said Jack, "but I don't know if we're much further ahead."

"I think we've made some progress," said La Grande Sauterelle. "Now we have to think a little. Let's go outside for a walk."

They reread Jacques Cartier's text, then slowly left the main hall, stopping here and there to glance at the objects in the exhibition. They paid special attention to a very large and beautiful map of North America on which one could see the vast territory that belonged to France in the mid-eighteenth century, a territory that extended from the Arctic to the Gulf of Mexico and west as far as the Rocky Mountains: it was an astonishing and very moving sight. But there was also an equally impressive map that depicted North America before the arrival of the whites; the map was strewn with the names of Indian tribes, names the man knew — Cree, Montagnais, Iroquois, Sioux, Cheyenne, Comanche, Apache — but also a large number of names he'd never heard of in his life: Chastacosta, Shuman, Miluk, Waco, Karankawan, Timucuas, Potanos, Yuchi, Coahuitlecan, Pascagoula, Tillamook, Maidu, Possepatuck, Alsea, Chawashas, Susquehanna, Calusa.

The girl stood for a long time in front of the second map. Her eyes were wet and shining, and Jack realized it was best to leave her alone for a moment. He returned to the lobby. The cleaning woman had nearly finished washing the floor. The man shook her hand and thanked her for the information.

"If you want to rest," she said, "you can go and sit in the library. It's the best place to get some peace and there're all sorts of books that talk about Jacques Cartier, if that's what interests you."

"Thanks again, *chère Madame*," he said.

"It's not often people call me that," she said with a broad smile.

"I'm going to get some air, then I'll come back and see the library."

LA GRANDE SAUTERELLE had brought the cat and they walked in silence to the edge of the strip of land that jutted out into the bay.

"Put yourself in Théo's place," she said.

They were in a birch wood, the man's favourite tree. The girl went on. "You come and visit the museum and then, for some reason or other, you get an urge to send a postcard with that account by Jacques Cartier you've just read in the main hall as the message. So what do you do?"

"I buy a postcard at the counter," he said.

"Right. And then?"

"Then I take the text to a printer and ask him to reproduce it on the postcard, but there's one hitch . . ."

"Obviously you can't bring him the poster from the main hall."

"Obviously."

"So."

He shrugged.

"It's simple," she said. "You go to the library."

"Why?"

"To get the book the text is taken from. And when you find it you make a photocopy and you take that to the printer."

"Sounds logical," he said.

He gave her a curious look.

"I don't know how you manage to have such clear ideas," he said. "My head's full of a sort of permanent fog and everything's all muddled up."

A few minutes later, Jack was in the library. The girl had stopped in the lobby to have a word with the cleaning woman, who was leaving. The library was small but well lit, and it had a large table, upholstered chairs and a card file of titles and authors. The man selected a number of books about Jacques Cartier's voyages and sat at one end of the table to consult them. Through the open door he could see the girl and the woman embracing, talking very softly. The girl was much taller than the woman, but their hair was exactly the same colour.

He skimmed several books and had just found the text by Jacques Cartier when La Grande Sauterelle came in. He showed her the text, which was on page 43 of a book by Joseph-Camille Pouliot, *La Grande Aventure de Jacques Cartier*, with the following note: "Facsimile taken from the original account of Cartier's 1st voyage, containing a description of the erection of a cross in the Baie de Gaspé, 24 July 1534."

"I like that man Pouliot a lot!" declared the girl.

"He was a judge," said Jack.

"Well then, thank you, Your Honour!"

She sat at the other end of the table and began to ruminate. Suddenly she stood up.

"I've got an idea," she said cheerfully.

"Another one?"

"We're going to conduct a little experiment, my dear Watson!"

She took the book and led Jack out of the library. At the information counter the young man was drinking a cup of coffee and smoking a cigarette.

She placed the open book in front of him.

"I'd like to have a photocopy of the facsimile."

"A photocopy of *what*?"

"This text."

She put her finger on it. He looked very closely at the round, eccentric handwriting of Jacques Cartier.

"Funny, I feel as if I've seen that somewhere . . ."

"You're very observant," she said.

"Thanks," he said. "Unfortunately there's no photocopier in the museum."

"No?"

"No."

"So how do you get photocopies?"

"I have no idea."

She did not despair, but asked, "Are you a student?"

"Yes. Why?"

"There's a photocopier at your school, isn't there?"

"Naturally."

"So what's to stop me from taking out this book and having the photocopy done at your school?"

"Nothing," he said.

He reflected and added, "You can take a book out of the museum as long as you put your name and address in the visitors' book."

"I don't understand," said the girl, a hint of emotion in her voice. "Did you say: 'In the book . . .?'"

"... The visitors' book," the young man repeated.

Jack and the girl looked at each other.

The young man took the book from a drawer and, opening it to the page for that day, placed it in front of her without a word.

She wrote her name and address at the spot he pointed to.

"What do you do with the old books, from past years?" she asked him next.

"We keep them," he said. "We put them in a filing cabinet."

"Of course. A museum's intended for keeping old things ..."

She had leaned her elbows on the counter, right across from him, and now she gave him a radiant smile.

"Could we have a look at the old books, if it's not too much trouble?"

He seemed to be wondering if she'd lost her mind.

II

The Legend of Eldorado

They were driving along Highway 132.

It was midafternoon. The May sun warmed the inside of the Volkswagen. The cat was lying in the glove compartment, asleep. The road followed the coastline of the Gulf of St. Lawrence. They scaled promontories and descended sharply to the tips of coves. They took turns at the wheel, intending to drive as far as Quebec, where the man lived, that day if possible.

They had left several villages behind them: Cap-des-Rosiers, Rivière-aux-Renards, l'Anse-à-Valleau. Jack was driving. He didn't say much because the countryside was beautiful, but at each village he couldn't help repeating how surprised he had been to see Théo's address in the visitors' book.

"I mean, really — St. Louis, Missouri!" And he added, "It's not even a complete address!"

He didn't understand. St. Louis, Missouri. No, really . . . Why that city rather than another? Why not New York? Why not Miami or Vancouver or even Los Angeles? He didn't even know exactly where St. Louis was. In fact, he knew nothing about the city, aside from the names of a few sports teams: the Cardinals in baseball, the Blues in hockey . . .

La Grande Sauterelle rummaged in the pocket behind the driver's seat. Amid an amazing assortment of road maps that had belonged to the previous owner of the van, she found a map of the United States. With a felt pen she traced what appeared to be the most usual route between Gaspé and St. Louis.

"Look at that," she said. "Does it suggest anything special?"

She folded the map in half and laid it on the steering wheel while the man was driving, and he could see that the route followed the St. Lawrence, passed through Quebec City and Montreal, made its way through the Great Lakes, then headed due south, going down the Mississippi to St. Louis.

"It reminds me of something," he said, "but it's rather vague . . ."

He hesitated.

"Something you've seen in old Canadian history books?" she insisted.

"That's it. A picture that showed the first French explorations in America. Was that . . . ?"

"Yes, that's what I was thinking of."

They arrived at Anse-Pleureuse.

In the village Jack parked the Volks by the side of the road, and they got out to stretch their legs and give the cat a chance to do what he hadn't done since morning.

They walked along the shore. They talked about Théo and the man recalled some stories from the childhood he and his brother had spent in a large frame house by a river, not far from the American border; then he touched on some of the exploits of the discoverers and explorers of the New World: Champlain, Etienne Brûlé, Jean Nicolet, Radisson, Louis Jolliet and Père Marquette,

Cavelier de La Salle, d'Iberville and La Vérendrye.

Abruptly the girl's face became impassive and her expression grew sad and obstinate. They returned to the Volkswagen. The cat got back in the glove compartment.

LA GRANDE SAUTERELLE gave the impression that she had spent her whole life at the wheel of a Volkswagen van. To climb hills, she would get a good start, shift down just as the motor was beginning to strain, accelerate as she got to the top and then start the descent in fourth, taking on speed until, on the approach to a curve, she pumped the brakes to reduce the speed of the motor and shifted down into third to harness the compression force.

"I really like the way you drive," said Jack. "Where did you learn?"

Looking glum, the girl peered at the road without a word. A few minutes later, however, she replied that she had learned from her father.

"He was a trucker," she said. "He drove trucks along the North Shore and at James Bay. When I was little he'd sit me on his knee and let me drive. Once he was sick and I drove a ten-ton Mack from Baie Comeau to Manicouagan. At first he watched and gave me advice, but then he lay down on the seat, wrapped in a blanket, and went to sleep . . . When he woke up we were at the fifth Manicouagan dam!"

"And how old were you?"

"Fifteen."

He whistled. She smiled briefly, but at once her face closed up again.

"Is something wrong?" he asked.

"It's hard to explain," she said. "But I'll try. I was born at La Romaine, on the North Shore. My mother's a Montagnais. She's the woman you saw at the Gaspé museum."

"And?"

"When you talk about the discoverers and explorers of

America . . . I've got nothing in common with the people who came looking for gold and spices and a passage to Asia. I'm on the side of the people who were robbed of their lands and of their way of life. And . . ."

She stopped to look at a freighter travelling down the river.

"And apparently the Indians came from Asia and reached America by means of an ice bridge that used to cover the Bering Strait. We came from the West and you came from the East. There's 7,000 kilometres between us!"

All at once she burst out laughing.

"Excuse me," she said. "I was starting to take myself seriously! Anyway, I'm not a real Indian. My father's white. I'm a Métis."

The girl laughed again, but her laughter was beginning to ring false.

Then the man announced, "I'm going to tell you a story."

"What story?" she asked, wiping her eyes.

"The story of Eldorado."

He cleared his throat a couple of times, and began. "On the high plateaus of the Andes in South America, two thousand three hundred metres above sea level, in a region unknown to white men that was called Cundinamarca or 'the land of the Condor,' a solemn ceremony was held every year. The chief of an Indian tribe would shed all his clothes, coat his body with a resinous substance, and roll in powdered gold. When he stood up, the sun made his gilded body glow, and he would march at the head of his tribe to the shore of a lake ringed by mountains, Lake Guatavita. There he got into a dugout canoe that took him to the middle of the lake, where he dove into the water. All the members of the tribe, even those who had stayed behind on shore, marvelled at the luminous gleam produced by the body of their chief, the gold-covered man, *el hombre dorado*, when he dove into the pure water of the lake. They talked about it among themselves, overcome with admiration, and word spread from tribe to tribe and from region to region, farther and farther, that somewhere in

America there existed a rich, mysterious land that was the kingdom of gold, *Eldorado*. And that's it. That's how the legend of Eldorado was born."

"It's a wonderful story," said the girl.

"Thank you," he said. "Didn't you know it?"

"No."

"I read it in Chapman's book, *The Golden Dream*."

And he couldn't help adding, somewhat sadly, "Everything I know, or just about, I've learned from books."

III

A Phone Call from Sam Peckinpah

"What do you do when you aren't looking for your brother?" asked La Grande Sauterelle.

"I'm a writer," said the man. "What are you?"

"A mechanic," she said. "I studied automobile mechanics."

"Do you have a diploma?"

"No. You?"

"Me neither," he said, smiling.

Despite their fatigue, they were happy to be in Quebec City. They had taken the ferry at Lévis. Leaning over the rail on the upper deck, they looked out at the lights of the Château Frontenac and Dufferin Terrace slowly coming toward them. Jack had a blanket around his shoulders. The girl, barefoot as usual, said she wasn't cold. When they were fairly near the north shore, he pointed out the house where his apartment was. It was to the left of the Château.

"The second house," he said. "Can you see it?"

"No," said the girl. "I just see a big black space."

"That's the Parc des Gouverneurs. But a little farther, to the left, there's a house that's lit up . . ."

"Yes."

"That's the American consulate. Then there's a house with a light on on the top floor."

The girl drew near and rested her head on his shoulder to get a better look at the lighted spot he was pointing to.

"Oh, yes, I see it now!" She asked, "Does that mean there's someone home?"

"No, I leave the light on because . . ." He gestured vaguely. "But there's no one there," he said.

The boat was approaching the wharf. They returned to the minibus, and after the gangplank had been lowered, they drove off the ferry and the old Volks struggled up the Côte de la Montagne. They drove around the Place d'Armes and under the arches of the Château, then found a parking spot at the end of the rue Terrasse-Dufferin, a stone's throw from the house where the man lived. Taking a few belongings and the cat, they climbed the five flights of stairs, careful not to make any noise because it was half-past four in the morning.

The apartment had only three rooms: living room, kitchen and bedroom, but the half-moon window in the living room, which had a window seat that could hold two people comfortably, offered a sweeping view of the river, the south shore and even the bridge to the Ile d'Orléans.

"There's no box for the cat," said the man.

"It doesn't matter," said the girl, who was sitting on the broad window seat. "We'll make do with newspapers for tonight."

"Do you want to go to bed right away?"

"No."

"I'll sleep on the sofa."

She gave no reply. She was looking outside, and her gaze was lost in the night. He came up to her.

"I'm going to make some hot chocolate. Would you like a cup?"

"Oh, yes," she said.

"Tired?"

"Not too. I'm waiting for daybreak, then I'll sleep for a while."

In the kitchen, he heated milk and poured a small amount into a saucer for the cat, who was rubbing against his legs. When the chocolate was ready, he brought the two cups into the living room; he set one down beside the girl, then sat facing her, at the other end of the window, with his legs folded under him.

She sipped it, then said, "It's very good."

"Thank you."

She asked: "Tell me some more about Théo."

He started to talk about his brother, and almost at once, a wave of memories swept him back to the frame house by the river, not far from the American border.

He began by describing the house, a stately square building two storeys high with three cellars, an attic and two sheds; on the second floor on the south side, there was a large glassed-in porch where the sun warmed anyone who came there to read or daydream or trade secrets.

The house, he said, was not right on the river, but about a kilometre away, and the most exciting way to travel that distance in winter was to slide across the frozen surface of a stream that ran near the house and flowed into the river; the stream had no name and it was underground: it ran under the garden, under the neighbour's garage, under a vacant lot, under a tennis court and under the main road, and it was a terrifying adventure to be flat on your stomach on a sled in the dark, icy tunnel where you would quickly gather speed and, if you deviated even slightly from the route Théo had laid out, risk smashing your head against a rock or being swallowed up by one of the eddies in the stream that had no name.

Théo enjoyed risky games. One of his favourites consisted of being pulled on skis by the neighbour's snowmobile. A huge character overflowing with energy, the neighbour was a doctor, and in winter, when the roads were closed by blizzards, he would use a snowmobile to call on patients who lived far from the village. "Doctor Noël's got out his snowmobile," people would say when they heard the dreadful racket the machine made as it crossed the village, sending up clouds of snow. The snowmobile, made of plywood, was shaped like a small automobile — a coupé — and was driven on two broad pairs of skis by an airplane propeller motor on the back. Whenever the doctor had some free time, Théo would don his downhill-ski equipment and have himself pulled along the river, clinging to a long cable. He could hold on for hours, indifferent to cold and fatigue, intoxicated by the frantic speed of the snowmobile that kept backfiring and giving the impression it might take off at any moment like an airplane.

La Grande Sauterelle was looking out the window as she sipped her chocolate; from where she sat, with pillows wedged against her back, she could get a glimpse of the lights on the bridge to the Ile d'Orléans.

Jack talked about the river a little more. Many of the memories that he shared with his brother were associated with that river. The memories had no precise age (he couldn't recall the exact year), but they were always associated with a season, and most often it was winter. He remembered, for instance, something from very long ago: men were using a saw to cut blocks of ice out of the river, and those blocks of ice, stored under piles of sawdust, kept the food in household iceboxes cold during the summer. He also remembered that they would clear a circular skating rink on the river and that, to warm skaters and provide light for them at night, they would burn old tires in the middle of the circle. He remembered that he and his brother used to go into the forest on the other side of the river, where they would catch rabbits with brass-wire snares. He remembered . . .

The girl's head had dropped to her shoulder, and the man saw that she had fallen asleep. He hesitated briefly, then wakened her as gently as he could, and they turned in for the night, the girl to the big bed and he to the sofa. The man had trouble getting to sleep, but it had been that way for a long time. When he woke up in midafternoon, the girl wasn't there. Or the cat.

In the kitchen sink he found the dishes she had used for breakfast, and they were the only traces of her in the apartment; she hadn't left a note to say where she had gone or whether she'd be back. He looked out the window to see if she was walking along Dufferin Terrace, but she wasn't there. When he leaned out he could see the old Volks at the end of the street; perhaps the girl's knapsack was still in the van, but he didn't really feel like going to look. He had a shower and something to eat, then started making a list of what he'd need for the journey to St. Louis. When he ran out of things to write down he felt like going for a stroll, so he went out, leaving the door unlocked.

The sky was grey, but it wasn't cold, and a fair number of people were walking in Old Quebec. The man crossed the park diagonally, then went along rue Haldimand and the slopes of the old city led him to the Librairie Garneau. Inside the bookstore, he studied the display of recently published novels and opened a few to read the first sentence, but nothing he read satisfied his requirements: the first sentence, he felt, should always be an invitation that no one could resist — a door opening on to a garden, the smile of a woman in a strange city. Then he went to the back of the store where the Québécois books were kept, and after checking that the clerks weren't watching, he looked for his own books on the shelves. He had written five novels, two of which were, by and large, failures. Strangely he found only the two novels he didn't like, and he opened one of them: the first sentence struck him as anything but an irresistible invitation. He replaced the book on its shelf and, before he left, bought the most recent road map of the United States.

He went home by way of rue Desjardins, so he could buy milk, butter and bread. Just as he was opening the door to his fifth-floor apartment, he heard the sound of dishes. He knocked before entering. La Grande Sauterelle was back.

"*Bonjour!* I bought a few things at the grocery store," he said as lightly as possible.

"So did I," said the girl.

"Oh, yes? What did you buy?"

"Milk, butter and bread," she said.

"Me too!" he laughed.

He went to the kitchen to put away his purchases. Then he got down on his knees and petted the cat, who was drinking some milk.

"Thanks for washing the dishes," he said.

"You're welcome," said the girl.

"And I'm glad you're back."

"Did you think I'd gone for good?"

"I didn't know what had happened. I looked to see if you'd left a note, but you hadn't."

"I couldn't," she said, "because . . ."

She unfastened the long braid that fell to the middle of her back, then she asked if he had a hairbrush. He went to get the brush from the medicine chest.

". . . I never know ahead of time what I'm going to do," she said.

He sat on the edge of the bed. The girl had her back to him. Standing at the window, legs slightly parted, she was brushing her hair. She untangled it with delicate strokes, starting at the bottom, then she bent her head to the left and brushed with long, regular strokes, over and under, then finally she shook her head until her long black hair enfolded her shoulders like a fur cape.

When she turned around she saw that the man was watching her, wide-eyed and openmouthed.

"Anything wrong?" she asked.

"No, no, everything's fine," he said.

He struggled to regain his self-control.

"Was there a phone call for me?" he asked.

"No," she said. "Are you expecting one?"

He nodded.

This girl was strange. Though he didn't know her very well, he felt very close to her and he felt that she was very close to him. He couldn't lie to her. He told her that he was expecting a call from Sam Peckinpah.

For action films, Sam Peckinpah was his favourite filmmaker. He had liked *Straw Dogs* very much. He had been captivated from the first images; the action had got faster and faster and he had been carried away by the rhythm of the film up to the moment when the word END appeared in big letters on the screen. He had left the cinema breathless and as tired as if he'd run a four-minute mile. Since that day, he had maintained the insane hope that old Peckinpah would call to tell him that he'd read his latest novel and wanted to make a film of it. Someday the phone would ring, he'd pick it up and, at the other end, he'd hear Peckinpah's gruff, nasal voice. It was ridiculous and illogical for all sorts of reasons, the main one being that he didn't write action novels and besides, he wasn't even a well-known author . . . But every time the telephone rang in his small fifth-floor apartment on the rue Terrasse-Dufferin, he told himself in spite of everything that maybe this, at last, was the phone call from Sam Peckinpah.

IV

The Ideal Writer

It was Saturday.

No question of starting out for St. Louis until the following week: Jack had to go to the bank, then take the Volks to the garage for an oil change and tune-up.

La Grande Sauterelle was still at his place. She hadn't said whether she would go with him or not. She didn't talk very much. She read. The girl read with a voracity he'd never seen before. In two days she had read everything he had written (she hadn't made any comment), then she read a novel by John Irving, *The Hotel New Hampshire*, in one day (she liked the character Susie the bear very much). When she went out she always took a book, which she put, along with the cat, into a small knapsack.

The girl had "borrowed" John Irving's book from the municipal library. When it came to getting books, she made a distinction between bookstores and libraries. From bookstores, she *stole* books quite unscrupulously, because in her opinion most booksellers were far more interested in money than in books; from libraries, however, she *borrowed* them: that is, she would slip them under her clothes or into her knapsack, then return them by mail after she had read them, including a brief note that read more or less as follows:

> Dear Librarian, I'm sending you this book which I happened to find in the bathroom at a service station in Sainte-Anne-de-la-Pocatière. I have no idea how it got there, but if I can give you some advice, I think you should take better care of your books. Signed: A Friend Who Wishes You Well, Pitsémine.

"Pitsémine" was La Grande Sauterelle's name in the Montagnais language. As for the writer, his pseudonym was Jack Waterman. One day he had asked his brother to suggest a pen name, and Théo had said he could think of nothing better than Waterman.

While La Grande Sauterelle devoured every book she could get her hands on, Jack Waterman was an anxious, parsimonious reader. He had his favourite authors, all of whose books he had read, but those authors were few in number: Hemingway, Réjean Ducharme, Gabrielle Roy, Salinger, Boris Vian, Brautigan and a few others. And he had his favourite books, which he reread frequently, and which were like old friends. In general, he felt no need to read during the periods when he was writing a novel; at those times, which were lasting longer and longer, other people's books made him impatient and sometimes even jealous.

For the time being, he had no novel in the works. He was experiencing those moments of anguish that await writers after they've finished a book and, already aware of its flaws and still unable to imagine the next book, they begin to doubt their talent. But as he wasn't writing, he could read, and since he was constantly thinking about his brother, he looked for books that had something to do with the journey to St. Louis.

That Saturday night, around nine o'clock, Jack was lying on the bed. They had returned from a walk along rue Saint-Jean, rue d'Auteuil and the Plains of Abraham, and they had come back to the apartment by way of the wooden staircase that descended to the terrace in stages, hugging the walls of the Citadel and the cliff at Cap Diamant; there was an impressive view of the river from the top of that staircase. The man suddenly got up and began searching through his bookcase. He muttered at the disorder that prevented him from finding the book he was looking for.

"What sort of book?" asked La Grande Sauterelle, who was sitting in her favourite corner of the window seat.

"A blue one," said Jack.

The bookcase was rather narrow, because the room was so cramped, but it went up to the ceiling. Planted in front of the shelves with his hands on his hips, he looked for the book.

"What's the title?" asked the girl.

"*The Exploration of the American Continent* or something like that," he replied, climbing up on a chair. "If I remember correctly, it should be somewhere near the top. I really ought to tidy up my books."

The girl got up.

"The one by Brouillette?" she asked.

"Do you know it?"

"Of course. I read it to see what he said about the Indians. I've read quite a lot about the Indians."

"I can't lay my hands on it."

"Here it is," said the girl.

She took a book from the bottom shelf and showed it to him.

"It's not Exploration, it's *The Penetration of the American Continent by the French Canadians*."

"You're right. So it is!"

"And it's not blue," she said. "It's brick red."

"*I* should be brick red," said the man, getting down from his chair. "Now I'm so embarrassed I can't even remember why I wanted to reread it."

"I seem to remember there's a section about St. Louis . . . Just a minute."

She looked at the table of contents, turned a few pages, then read aloud:

> "Wherever trading was carried out, we find traces of French Canadians, pure blooded at the beginning of the period, later of mixed blood . . . We shall follow the traders from their principal centres of influence, which were in turn: Detroit, Michilimackinac, Grand-Portage (later Fort William) and St. Louis."

"Thank you," said Jack. "That's exactly the section I was looking for. I mean, I'd forgotten it, but it was still somewhere in my unconscious and I was trying to find it again."

La Grande Sauterelle went back to her favourite corner. She was reading a book by Gabrielle Roy, *The Fragile Lights of Earth*.

"Of course that doesn't explain why Théo was going to St. Louis," she said, before she returned to her book.

"No, it doesn't."

"All it means is that St. Louis was a trading post."

A moment later she continued, "But everybody knows that the trading posts were located along waterways . . . so they weren't used just for the fur trade: they were also starting points for all sorts of expeditions."

" . . . All sorts of expeditions?" he repeated, in the hope that she would add something.

The girl knew far more than he did about history and perhaps even about Théo's motivations.

"It will be easier to understand after we're in St. Louis," she said, becoming engrossed in her reading.

"So you're coming?" he asked.

She did not reply. When something was self-evident she never replied. He lay down on the bed again and started leafing through Brouillette's book. He wasn't really in the mood to read, but he turned the pages, stopping at certain passages that attracted his attention.

The book talked a great deal about the *voyageurs*. The author seemed to think very highly of them. Jack wanted to know if the girl shared that feeling, and he read her the following passage:

> "By common consent, the Canadians are best able, in their role of paddlers, to tolerate the rigours of an expedition by canoe. It is rare for others to be used for such demanding work. As *voyageurs* the Canadians deserve the highest praise."

And farther on he read:

> "I have seen them paddle a canoe for twenty hours straight, travelling at that rate for a fortnight or three weeks without a day to rest or slow down."

La Grande Sauterelle said that she liked the *voyageurs* very much and she thought that if they'd been educated and if they had left any writings, their exploits would probably be compared with those of the pioneers of the American West. She also thought that they had behaved acceptably toward the Indians, given the customs of the time. Same thing for the trappers and the *coureurs de bois*: in general, they had treated the Indians better, in her opinion, than their American counterparts.

The man couldn't help smiling. He closed the book and crossed his hands behind his head, and the cat came and lay on his stomach and began to purr.

"Do you like the book by Gabrielle Roy?" he asked.

"Very much," said the girl in a voice that already seemed far away.

He would have liked to tell her that the title of Gabrielle Roy's took on a special significance when you knew that she was a very beautiful and very vulnerable woman and that her green eyes shone like lights. He would have liked to tell her, too, not to read too quickly, because Gabrielle Roy had a highly individual style and that, for example, it was always interesting to see where she placed the adverbs in her sentences.

But as he didn't want to interrupt the girl's reading again, he kept quiet. And so he was sent back to himself and to his own writing.

Jack Waterman was not very pleased with himself as a writer. He didn't like himself very much in general (he thought he was too thin and too old and too withdrawn), but what he hated about himself more than anything was his way of working. He had always had an image of the ideal writer, and he was utterly unlike that model. He ranked himself with those whom he called "the industrious class": patient and persistent but bereft of inspiration or even impulses, he went to work at the same time every day and, thanks to methodical and dogged work habits, managed to turn out his daily page.

Here is what he imagined the ideal writer to be like and the terms in which he talked about him:

ONE FINE EVENING, the ideal writer is sitting in the back room of the Sainte-Angèle Bar, when all at once he gets an idea for a novel. He hasn't written a novel for two years perhaps, and that night, as he sips a Tia Maria with friends in a bar in Old Quebec, this idea comes to him out of the blue.

The idea is far-ranging, yet precise, with two very clear-cut characters, the plot, the tone — even the first sentence!

He says *excuse me* and goes up to the bar. He borrows a pen from the barmaid. He writes the first sentence on a paper napkin.

But then the second sentence comes to him, and he writes it on the other side of the napkin. It's longer than the first one, but it, too, is all thought out, and he has no trouble writing it; and the tone is exactly right.

Just as the writer is about to go back to his friends, a third sentence comes to him, but there's no room left on the napkin. He's afraid he'll forget it, and he repeats it in his head several times. He senses it going away . . . He has a terrible memory. He rummages in his pockets, looking for a scrap of paper, but he finds nothing, so finally he writes the sentence in abbreviated form on a matchbook that's lying on the bar.

He leaves the Sainte-Angèle, waving a vague goodbye to his friends. One of them catches up with him on the street.

"Anything wrong? Don't you feel well?"

The writer shakes his head.

"Shall I take you home?" asks the friend.

He nods.

The friend has him get in his car and drives him home. He asks if he needs anything.

"Five writing pads."

"*Five* pads?"

"Yes, five!" he says impatiently.

"Lined or unlined?"

The question sounds like the stupidest thing he has ever heard. He glares at his friend, who says nothing more and leaves at once.

The writer sets to work.

He begins by transcribing the first three sentences on to an old pad and all three stand up; they are well constructed, and at the end of the third comes another, then another. The ideas are jostling one another in his head; they come faster and faster, and he wonders if he will be able to keep up the rhythm. Then he takes a sheet of paper and jots down, as they occur to him, the ideas that will be useful later. And then he goes back to his writing. It's pleasant and comforting to have ideas in reserve. He

writes with a sort of feverish pleasure. Words and sentences come easily, and the source seems inexhaustible. He has the impression that someone is dictating what he has to write. He feels very good. He is writing at full speed, and he is living intensely . . . . .
. . . .

The sound of a voice nearby makes him start.

His friend has come back.

The writer didn't hear the door . . . Nor did he understand what the other man said, but he found some writing pads . . . That's it, he said something like, "I had to go all the way to Lower Town. Lippen's Drugstore."

"Thank you," he said. "Now please go away."

"I'm going to sleep here," says the friend.

"Leave me alone!"

"Listen, it's four a.m.!"

"SCREW OFF!"

The friend gets the point. He leaves. He doesn't look very happy, but he goes. Just before he shuts the door, the writer says, "Tell Marie not to come tomorrow."

"Okay."

"Or the day after, either! Tell her not to disturb me."

His friend goes out and he starts writing again.

To immerse himself in the atmosphere again, he rereads the previous page, and at once the words start coming! His friends the words are there when he needs them. They arrive *en masse*, pushing one another to make room. He is very glad to see them, and he writes like a madman, a maniac. He no longer knows what time it is, whether it is day or night. His characters argue, they act, they make decisions, and he has a strong sense that he is a spectator in this story and that his role consists of describing as faithfully as possible the action that is taking place before his eyes. The characters know precisely where they are going and they take him along with them into a New World . . . .
. . . .

Fog.

Everything is white.

He hears a far-off voice: "Jack! Jack Waterman!"

A face is bending over him. Marie.

"*Bonjour*," she says.

The walls are white. He is in a bed.

He tries to get up but cannot. He can hardly move his head. He is very tired.

"Everything's fine," says Marie. "Don't move." She takes his hand and raises it gently so he can see: a transparent plastic tube is attached to the back of his hand; beside the bed, a flask of serum is hanging from a stand.

A nurse comes into the room and busies herself taking his blood pressure.

"Glad to see you back with us!" she says, smiling.

He makes an effort to ask what has happened, but no sound emerges from his mouth. And suddenly he remembers: THE NOVEL! THE SHEETS OF PAPER SCATTERED OVER THE TABLE AND FLOOR . . . then a great black space . . .

"Stay calm," says the nurse.

"Wait a minute," says Marie.

She opens a drawer in the little chest beside his bed and takes out a binder. A very big one.

"Don't talk," says the nurse. "You've been unconscious for three days and you mustn't tire yourself. Understand?"

He nods and looks at Marie, because he needs to know. She is bending over him, holding the manuscript against her chest and looking intently at him.

She says, "The writing's hard to decipher, especially at the end, but . . ."

There are tears in her eyes when she says, "It's the most beautiful story I've ever read!"

V

The Thousand Islands

They were in Ontario and had been driving along Highway 401 for two hours.

"First exit on the right," said La Grande Sauterelle, looking up from the assortment of road maps and brochures in her lap, which they had been given by the *Club Automobile de Québec.*

She pointed to a sign that announced the town of Rockport. Jack flicked on the turn signal and took the exit she had pointed to. Why the girl was asking him to leave the highway and head for Rockport he had no idea, but she was an excellent navigator. She had an unerring sense of direction, she always consulted several maps and she studied not only the road they were to follow, but also the entire region through which they would travel.

"I've never seen the Thousand Islands," she said. "We'll take the road that follows the river. It's just a tiny little detour and we can stock up on supplies in Rockport, then go on to Ivy Lea. There's a provincial campground at Ivy Lea. Is that all right with the pilot?"

"Absolutely," said the man. "Anyway, the pilot's tired of driving on a four-lane highway. Is it very far to Rockport?"

"We're nearly there."

They were driving along a tree-lined road that went right to the river. Not far from a wharf where two glass-bottomed excursion boats were moored, they spotted an old general store. The girl picked up her cat and went and sat at the end of the wharf to look at the islands, while the man went into the store and bought a can of bluefish and the ingredients for a fish salad.

Then they got back on the road that followed the river and drove to Ivy Lea.

The campground was divided into two sections, and the one that looked out on the river was wilder, almost deserted, so they chose a spot there; they were at the water's edge and isolated from any possible neighbours by a row of conifers.

Jack prepared the meal by himself. The girl was busy looking at the river and the islands. There were all sorts of islands, big and small, and they were all inhabited, even the very smallest. Just across from the campground there was a tiny island completely covered by a house on stilts. Somewhere in the middle of the river an imaginary boundary divided Canada and the United States.

La Grande Sauterelle wolfed down her bluefish salad without saying a word and without interrupting her reverie. Later, she seemed not to notice that it had grown dark, that there were mosquitoes and that it was becoming cool and damp.

She didn't answer when Jack said that he understood now why the other campers had chosen the section farther from the river: they wanted to avoid the mosquitoes, and also their section had outlets so they could hook up a heater inside their trailers.

"I'm going to make a fire," said the man.

He began to collect dead branches.

"What are you thinking about?" he finally asked the girl.

"I'm not thinking," she said softly. "I'm dreaming."

She turned her head toward him, and from his woeful look she realized he was feeling rejected. He had driven the Volkswagen all afternoon, he had made a good bluefish salad, with fresh fruit for dessert and coffee, he had washed the dishes and put everything back in the minibus. And now he was gathering dead branches to make a fire and drive the mosquitoes away.

"Dreams are like islands," she murmured. "You're all alone when you dream, and that's how it has to be. Do you understand?"

He nodded and she explained, "I was dreaming of the great birchbark canoes."

In her dream there were not just the Indians' canoes, but also the big canoes, ten to twelve metres long, made by the *voyageurs* for the fur trade on the St. Lawrence and the Great Lakes; known as *canots du maître*, they had fourteen-man crews. Of course not all the canoes were that big. Most measured around eight metres long; they were very elegant, pointed at both ends and could accommodate a dozen men. The frame was made of narrow white cedar laths, and the hull of birchbark strips sewn together; spruce gum was used to caulk the seams. Once they were completed, they cut a proud figure with the thwarts, the seats, the paddles and the coloured decorations, and they glided silently across the water, laden with furs, provisions or trade goods to be delivered at posts such as Detroit or Michilimackinac.

"Detroit or what?" asked Jack. "Michilimackinac," she said.

"Michili . . . what?"

He had understood perfectly well, and in any case, it was a name he had long been familiar with, but she had a very special way of pronouncing it.

"Michilimackinac!" she repeated.

The way she pronounced it made all the vowels ring out, while the last syllable made a slapping sound like the flat of a paddle striking the water. The man had an inordinate passion for words, and he almost believed that this girl could utter a magic word that would cause to appear before their eyes a convoy of great canoes that would thread their way among the islands, then dissolve into the night, raising behind them a swell so strong that it could make the island lights, which had just come on and were reflected in the calm river water, dance and dance.

Sitting on a big log with her back to the campfire, La Grande Sauterelle looked out at the illuminated houses on the islands. Jack sat beside her. The fire warmed their backs and it felt pleasant, but it had no effect on the mosquitoes. The man rose and tossed some green boughs and handfuls of wet grass on the fire, which started to smoke.

"I like the lights," said the girl.

"So do I," he said.

"I think nature's most beautiful when there's nothing there — I mean, when it's still the way it was in the beginning — but I like lights, too. I'm torn between the two and I know I always will be."

Her voice broke, and Jack could think of nothing to say. Suddenly the wind turned and blew the smoke their way. They moved their log to the other side of the campfire. A few moments later, the wind changed again, and they took the log back to the spot they'd just left. No sooner were they seated than the wind turned yet again and blew the smoke right at them. This time they refused to move.

"The wind's crazy," said the man. "In a minute it's going to change sides again."

Half stifled by the smoke, eyes watering, they obstinately stayed on the log. The wind didn't turn.

"I have an idea," said the girl in an undertone. "Let's pretend we're changing sides, so . . ."

"Sshhh!" he said.

They got up, and positioned at either end of the log, they made as if they were going to lift it and move it to the other side of the fire. They stayed like this for a good minute, knees flexed and backs bent, but the wind, as if it understood their ruse, kept blowing in the same direction. Finally they gave up and took shelter inside the Volkswagen.

It was as cold inside as out.

Jack switched on the ceiling light and, to warm himself, hoisted into the "attic" all the baggage in the back of the Volks. The "attic" was the compartment just under the roof, which was enlarged when the roof was raised. When the baggage was placed up here, the back of the Volks was totally cleared and the seat could be pulled down to make a bed for two. The man stowed all their belongings in the "attic" except for the sleeping bags, blankets and the suitcase that contained their warm clothes.

"Are you cold?" he asked.

"A little," she said. "It's the damp . . . Isn't there a gas heater in the Volks?"

"Yes, but it's never worked very well. It gives off a strong smell of gas and . . ."

"So we have a choice between death by freezing and asphyxiation?"

"I'm really sorry."

"It doesn't matter. I'll get in my sleeping bag."

"I thought Indians were never cold . . ."

"I told you, I'm not a real Indian," she cut in, and muttered something that he didn't catch.

"I'm sorry," he said.

He spread a flannel blanket on the bed for insulation and to prevent unpleasant contact with the vinyl seat cover. Next, he unrolled the sleeping bags, undid the zippers and put the pillows inside, then spread a warm woollen blanket over the bags. He accomplished all this without a word, and, despite the cold, he did his best to be quick, precise and efficient, as if it were his mission to prepare the bed for Princess Kateri Tekakwitha herself.

When he had finished, he took some warm clothes from the suitcase: two pairs of wool socks, two sweaters, two tuques and two sets of pink Penmans long johns, made all in one piece, with a long row of buttons in front and a little flap, closed by a single button, in the back.

At the sight of the long johns the girl choked and was seized by uncontrollable giggles. She was still laughing when she started to take off her clothes and get into the sleeping bag.

The man turned his back.

"What are you doing?" she asked.

"Nothing. I'm turning away while you put on your long johns."

"I've already done it!"

He turned and saw that the girl was burrowed in the sleeping bag up to her neck. The two sets of long johns were still on the bed.

"I won't put them on unless I'm freezing to death," she said.

"It's up to you."

He got undressed without looking at the girl, hurrying because it was cold. He was rushing to button the front of his long johns when he realized that the girl was watching him.

"I just want to see how you look in them," she said.

"Well?"

"Turn around so I can . . ."

"I'm freezing," he said.

"I'm not in the least surprised."

"Why?"

"The little door, it's . . ."

"What?"

"The little door," she repeated. "It's open!"

He put his hand behind him to check, but everything was buttoned up and properly closed. The girl laughed even harder. He switched off the ceiling light and quickly got into his sleeping bag.

"The cat's with me," she said, "and if you get in, too, maybe the three of us will be able to get warm."

She pulled down the zipper and he moved closer to her, turning his back. She huddled against him, pressing her knees into the backs of his and resting her stomach against his back, then she wrapped one arm around his shoulder. He felt something soft and warm against his feet: it was the cat. He also felt a hard object digging into the small of his back, so he reached down and his fingers touched the elongated form of a small hunting knife in a leather sheath.

"Excuse me," said the girl. "I always forget to take it off."

She unfastened the cord that held the sheath around her waist and said that she always carried the knife on her since a misadventure she'd experienced on a trip; she didn't feel like talking about it just now.

"But I'm going to tell you a special story to thank you for everything you've done today," she said. "And it's also a story that will warm you up."

She told him she had read the story in a book called *The Secret Language of Animals*, and she collected her thoughts for a moment.

Then she began:

> "When winter is on its way in Antarctica, the king penguins do the opposite of other birds: instead of migrating to warm countries, they make their way to the ice floes that are found in the coldest regions of the globe. They go there every year to give birth to their young. After they've mated and the female has laid her egg, the male takes the egg and puts it in an incubating pouch on his belly. Then the female goes away. She bids farewell to the male and leaves the ice floe to go catch fish in open water. The males stay there all alone with their eggs and they don't eat a thing for eight long weeks, but they have invented a special system to protect themselves from the wind and the cold and the blowing

snow. They form a big circle, with the weakest ones in the middle, and the circle slowly turns on itself. When they've regained their strength and got warm again, the ones that had been in the middle give their places to the others, so that each one takes a turn at being exposed to the cold, then comes and takes shelter in the middle of the circle. That's how penguins that are about to become fathers manage to survive and protect themselves from the cold on the ice floes at the South Pole while they wait for their mates to return.

And that's it. That's the end of my story."

"I'm warm already," said Jack. "It's a fine story and you tell it very well."

"Thank you."

"I don't know if my brother's in St. Louis or somewhere else," he said, "but if he's at the South Pole I hope the penguins are encircling him and warming him."

"I hope so, too," she said.

"Good night!"

"Good night!"

VI

A Discussion About Etienne Brûlé

It was windy and rainy — it was even dangerous to drive the old Volks on the 401 — and as they didn't have the slightest desire to stay in a campground again, they decided to stop in Toronto and take a room at the YMCA.

The YMCA was located at 40 College Street. They had found the address in the literature from the Automobile Club, along with other information, in particular a reference that had caught Jack's attention, because it said that the first white man to explore the region that is now the city of Toronto had been Etienne Brûlé, in 1615. Etienne Brûlé was one of his brother's heroes.

La Grande Sauterelle said: "That doesn't mean that Théo . . ."

"I know, I know," he said.

When they were little, there was a big garden with trees, flowers, swings and a small gazebo beside the house; next to it was a wooden fence and a hedge of honeysuckle. The garden, along with the vacant lot to which you gained access through a wooden arch, was the setting for the endless battles waged every day after school that pitted the neighbourhood whites against the Indians.

THEY ENTERED THE YMCA and Jack asked for a room.

"Single or double?" asked the desk clerk.

He had spoken very fast, slurring the last word, and Jack thought the man wanted to know if he was single or married. The man had a bony face and a bald head, and he was wearing a white T-shirt and a plastic whistle hanging around his neck. He was looking suspiciously at the girl.

"Single," Jack replied after a brief hesitation.

"You don't seem sure."

"No, I'm sure," he said more firmly.

In the elevator, La Grande Sauterelle teased him. They had been given separate rooms, one on the second floor (reserved for female guests), the other on the fourth (the floor for male guests), rather than one room with twin beds on the third floor, where married people were put.

"Which floor?" she asked in English, pretending she didn't know him.

"Fourth," he replied, very vexed.

"I see," she went on in English. "You're single?"

He shrugged.

"You don't like women?"

She pulled her dress midway up her thighs.

"Are you sure?"

The elevator stopped at the second floor and the door opened, but La Grande Sauterelle refused to get out.

"You missed your floor," he said as the elevator started up again.

"I have a better idea," she said.

At the fourth floor, she got out with him and followed him to his room, which was at the end of a long corridor; he walked very fast to avoid being seen in her company.

The room was small: a single bed, a bureau with a lamp, a wooden chair and, in one corner, a washbasin with a medicine chest above it. They deposited on the bed their two suitcases and the canvas bag that contained the cat. From the window there was a fine view to the south, and they could see the City Hall, which resembled a gigantic pair of hands, curved and pointing to the sky.

"It must be gorgeous at night, with all the lights," said the girl.

She took off her dress.

THE SCHOOLBAGS lay abandoned at the foot of a tree.

Théo went into the gazebo and whites and Indians gathered around him. He was the oldest and the biggest and also the most learned, because he had read all sorts of books.

He told the story of Etienne Brûlé. He had a special way of telling it: with many gestures he mimed the events so that everyone could see how Etienne Brûlé, arriving in New France with Champlain, had obtained permission to live with the Indians so as to learn their language, and had become, at eighteen, the first *coureur de bois*; how he lived like the Indians, who adopted him as one of their own, and how he had led a number of expeditions into the Great Lakes region and had made his way south to Chesapeake Bay.

"WILL YOU LEND ME a pair of jeans?" asked the girl.

She was wearing nothing but her white underpants.

"Of course," said Jack.

"I'm going to disguise myself as a male guest," she said.

He avoided looking at her. He walked around the room, scratching his head, then rummaged in the canvas bag.

"Why don't you look in the suitcase," she suggested calmly.

"The suitcase? . . . Oh, yes, of course. I can't think straight."

The jeans were indeed in the suitcase. They were the right length, a bit loose around the waist, but with a belt they would do.

"They fit fine," she said.

She put her hands in the pockets and swiveled around to give him a look. The jeans were U.F.O. brand, and those letters appeared at the top of her right buttock.

"They look as if they were tailor-made for you," he said, exaggerating slightly.

She smiled.

"Can I ask you something else?"

"Of course," he said.

"Can't you guess?"

He shook his head.

She drew closer and stood facing him, hands on her hips.

"Can you see anything?"

"Nothing special," he said insistently.

"I need something to go with the jeans. A shirt or something."

"Why not a T-shirt like you usually wear?"

"Because of *these*," she said, pointing to her breasts. "I know they're small, but they still show, don't they?"

"Of course. As a matter of fact I could see them all the time, if you really want to know."

"So now you understand why I need a shirt," she said. "One with two pockets would be best. Then people would just think I have something in my pockets. Get it?"

Jack rummaged in his suitcase again. He found a long-sleeved, khaki shirt of military cut, which came from Latulippe Surplus de Guerre, and in fact it had two pockets in the front. The girl tried it on and it fit very well. Then she rolled her braid into a chignon. Without waiting for her to ask, he gave her a hat and tennis shoes. He expected that the "running shoes," as she called them, would be too wide for her long narrow feet, but they fit well, like the other clothes. She looked exactly like a boy.

"Shall we go for a walk?" she suggested, pushing her sleeves up to the elbow.

In the corridor she began to whistle. She stopped an old gentleman to ask him the time and he replied, "Four o'clock, sir."

AT A SIGNAL FROM THÉO the group split into two sections: whites and Indians.

While the whites were turning the garden into a fortress, the Indians withdrew to the back of the vacant lot, where they prepared for battle by covering their faces with "war paint" they'd taken from various tins of shoe polish; they filled their quivers with rubber-tipped arrows and performed a dance accompanied by war whoops. After that, the Indians crawled off behind the trees, along the fences, and under the honeysuckle hedge, then they stormed the fort, whooping hysterically. When the stock of arrows was exhausted and whites and Indians were reduced to hand-to-hand combat, Etienne Brûlé himself made his appearance and brought the confrontation to an end with a fantastic shot with the harquebus Champlain had lent him. And if Etienne Brûlé didn't intervene in the battle, it was Daniel Boone in his buckskin jacket, or Davy Crockett with his bizarre hat, or Sheriff Wild Bill Hickok, or even Buffalo Bill with his old Winchester.

ON LEAVING THE YMCA they turned left, because Yonge Street lay in that direction and also because the Toronto Reference Library was only a few blocks away and La Grande Sauterelle wanted to "borrow" a book.

"Are you thinking about your brother?" she asked.

"Yes," he said.

"That's not hard to see."

"Why?"

The girl did not reply.

"I don't know how you do it," said the man. "You always

seem to be thinking just about yourself . . . For instance, you're walking beside me, quite obviously enjoying the fact that people are taking you for a boy — but you still know what's going on in my mind."

They arrived at the library. The building had a forbidding look, but inside it was peaceful and friendly. There were galleries all around an enormous skylight, and everywhere there were rugs and plants and even a little fountain murmuring discreetly in the middle of a rock garden.

A security guard was standing at the front door, near the desk, and the girl asked him what floor the history books were on.

"*Au quatrième*," he told her in French.

They took the elevator to the fourth floor. They consulted the card catalogue and considered a number of books, until La Grande Sauterelle finally chose one entitled *Toronto During the French Regime*. A half hour later, when they decided to leave, the girl hid the book inside her shirt, holding it in place with her belt, but she couldn't resist the urge to test the vigilance of the security guard.

She went up to him, her arms crossed over the book.

"What year was this library built?" she inquired.

"About 1977," replied the guard.

He seemed to be about fifty and had a salt-and-pepper beard.

He spoke French with barely a trace of an accent.

"That's what I thought," she said, speaking to Jack. "*Théo* couldn't have been here. The library didn't exist."

"Théo's my brother," Jack explained. "We don't know where he is exactly, and we're looking all over. All we know is that he was in Gaspé about fifteen years ago, because we found his trail there, in a library. After that we think he went to St. Louis, Missouri."

"So he would have come through Toronto," added the girl.

"And you've tried to find his trail here?"

"Not really. I wanted to read a book about Etienne Brûlé," she said, uncrossing her arms in a gesture of defiance.

The guard looked her up and down, his gaze resting for a moment on the bulge in her shirt.

"I see you found what you were looking for," he said with a knowing smile.

"You aren't a *real* security guard, are you?" asked the girl.

"My actual work is doing research in philosophy," he said, "but times are tough and you have to earn a living, right? And anyway, I like books."

"I promise I'll mail it back," she said apologetically.

"Are you a professor?" asked Jack.

"Student," said the guard. "It may strike you as odd at my age, but that's how it is. I didn't realize that time was passing, as I've been studying all my life."

"Are you interested in history?"

"You have to know history if you want to be a good philosopher . . . But why do you ask?"

"I'd like to know what you think of Etienne Brûlé."

The guard stroked his beard pensively.

"Do you . . . do you hold him in special esteem?" he inquired cautiously.

"N . . . no, not exactly."

"Do you want an honest answer?"

"Of course."

"I think Etienne Brûlé was a bum."

"Aha!"

Jack stood with his mouth open for a moment and the man asked, "Don't you use that word in Quebec?"

"Oh, we use it, all right," said Jack.

"Did I say something I shouldn't have?"

"No, it's okay."

They thanked the man for his information and were about to take their leave when he added, "About your brother, perhaps you should go to police headquarters."

"What for?" asked Jack sharply. "Do you think my brother . . ."

"I don't mean that! You ought to go because they have excellent records, that's all. When I did some historical research, for instance, I found all sorts of interesting things in their files. If your brother stopped over in Toronto, they may have information on him. Sometimes you find just small details, but they can lead to important discoveries if you do some — how do you say "cross-checking" in French?"

"*Recoupements*," said Jack.

"That's right. Thanks."

"You're welcome. I'm very grateful for your help."

"I phoned police headquarters to tell them you were coming," said the man, shaking hands with them. "Good luck in your research!"

THEY WERE GREETED by a uniformed woman who hadn't quite understood the guard's call.

"You're trying to find a certain Etienne Brûlé, is that it?" she asked in laboured French.

Jack explained patiently that he was, rather, looking for his brother Théo and that the Etienne Brûlé in question was a *coureur de bois*.

"That's good!" said the woman. "There aren't many *coureurs de bois* left in Ontario. If there are any, they must be in Quebec."

They looked to see if she was joking, but no, she was quite serious. She showed them to the archives, in the basement. They were expecting to meet an old policeman close to retirement, but it was a very young man with smooth cheeks and an innocent look who greeted them. Jack gave him his brother's name, and the young policeman opened a drawer and began to flip through the files.

"Reference number 5289," he said, sticking a pencil in front of the file he had just discovered.

He muttered the number as he took them into another room, where he consulted a second file.

"We're in luck," he said.

"Why?" asked La Grande Sauterelle.

"Because there's a microfilm. Just a second . . ."

He rummaged around under a counter, took out a cassette, inserted it into a viewer and suggested they sit down.

"Do you know how it works?"

"Yes," said the girl.

He turned it on himself and then, stepping back, leaned over to take a look at the first image; it was somewhat blurred, and he turned a knob to adjust the focus.

"Is that all right?"

"Just fine," said Jack.

But the young policeman continued to look at the picture. La Grande Sauterelle turned to him.

"The image is perfect," she said firmly, and looked at him so insistently that he turned on his heel and went back into the other room.

The first image showed a general information sheet on which appeared Théo's name, his father's Christian name, his age (45), his date of birth, occupation (traveller) and the number of his driver's licence; under the heading "Nature of Complaint" were the words: "unlicensed firearm."

The next images reproduced an interrogation that dealt with two elements in particular:

A) To the question regarding his occupation, Théo had replied "traveller," and he was unable to explain to the policeman's satisfaction what that occupation consisted of and how it enabled him to earn his living.

B) The matter of the firearm did not go beyond mere "possession."

The final image showed a closeup of Théo's possessions:

- a revolver
- an old Camargue hat
- a stopwatch

- a wallet containing $32.58
- *On the Road* by Jack Kerouac
- a Swiss army knife
- a photograph of a girl, inscribed "Claudia, St. Louis"
- a book entitled *The Oregon Trail Revisited.*

THEY WENT BACK TO THE YMCA.

Jack had a nap while the girl read her book, then they took the cat and went out to grab a bite in a restaurant on Yonge Street. The girl was still wearing her boy's getup.

The man didn't talk very much.

"Tired?" asked the girl.

"A little," he said. "What about you?"

"I'm all right. And the cat's just fine, too."

She had ordered a club sandwich and a Coke, and she was feeding pieces of chicken to the cat, which was on her lap. The man was absently munching a hamburger and drinking a glass of milk.

"You don't eat very much," she said. "Are you worried about Théo because of the police record?"

"Tell me about Etienne Brûlé," he said by way of reply. "Does the author of your book think he was a bum?"

There was some anger in his voice, as well as a mixture of sorrow and fatigue, and the girl did not reply at once. She took the book from her canvas bag and started leisurely turning the pages.

"The author doesn't have a very high opinion of him," she began cautiously.

"Why? What did he do?"

"He . . . You know, when the Kirke brothers attacked Quebec in 1629 . . ."

"Yes. Then what?"

"He was the one who guided the English expedition on the St. Lawrence. He betrayed his country."

"That's a good start! And what else is he accused of?"

"He's reproached for the way he behaved with the Indians. The Indian women. He was always changing wives. The author says . . . Hold on. Oh, yes, here it is: 'He changed Indian wives as rapidly and as frequently as he changed his horizons in his restless roaming across the land.'"

"So what?" said the man.

"And Champlain says of him: 'This man was known to be highly licentious and much given to women.'"

"Champlain was very scrupulous, like everyone else at the time, don't you think?"

"Very likely," she said.

"And the Indians' sexual practices were more liberal than the whites', weren't they?"

"Yes. Obviously."

"As far as sex is concerned," he went on, "I think you should be allowed to do anything as long as you respect the other person's freedom."

"That's what I think, too," said the girl. "But in the case of Etienne Brûlé . . ."

She gave the cat a piece of chicken.

" . . . something happened, no one knows exactly what, but he did something that ran counter to the customs of the tribe he was living with, and the Indians . . . They ran out of patience and put him to death."

"Good God!" said Jack.

He looked stunned, like a man who has just received bad news about someone close to him.

"I'm so sorry," said the girl.

The man could think of nothing to say and shrugged. They went on eating in silence. When they had finished, the girl asked, "May I pretend to be a great psychologist?"

"Of course you may," he said dully.

"Its not Etienne Brûlé you're trying to defend, it's your brother Théo. You're afraid your brother's done something wrong . . . but since you don't like that idea, it's repressed in your unconscious, and instead of defending your brother, you're defending Etienne Brûlé."

Jack pondered for a moment.

"You may be right," he said. "I admit that, deep down, it's Théo I'm thinking about. I probably feel guilty about something. But what? It's hard to say because there's always this fog in my head . . ."

"You've said that before," said the girl, smiling. "Excuse me. Where was I?"

"You were saying you felt guilty . . ."

"Ah, yes. I feel guilty . . . of not helping my brother at a time when he needed me. At least, I think that's it."

He tried to explain to the girl how he saw things. The postcard that his brother had sent him from Gaspé — fifteen years ago — was a sort of cry for help, a distress signal. But he had not understood, for two reasons: first, at the time he was working on a novel, which kept him from paying attention to what was going on around him; second, Théo had made the message difficult to decipher because he was too proud to come right out and ask for help. He understood all that now, and he felt guilty at the thought that his brother had spent weeks in Gaspé, waiting, then went back on the road, probably hitchhiking, perhaps intending to go to St. Louis where he knew a girl called Claudia, and that he'd got into trouble with the police in Toronto because of the business with the revolver.

"And perhaps they put him in jail," the girl added.

"Why?" he asked, with no hostility this time.

"He didn't have enough to pay the fine," she said. "All he had on him was $32.58."

"That's true."

"But going to jail isn't all that serious. I did once, and my father's been several times."

"Oh yes?"

"And anyway, I think we're lucky to have found his trail again," she said. "After all, there are two and a half million people in Toronto."

"You're right. And I think you're a great psychologist."

"Thank you. You're a sweetheart."

"You're a sweetheart, too," he said. "You're very intelligent and very beautiful."

"And you're the handsomest man I've ever met."

She burst out laughing.

"And the two of us are the biggest liars in North America!" she said.

They were very cheerful when they left the restaurant. Yonge Street was starting to light up, and they strolled along the sidewalk, first in one direction, then the other, looking at the people and the store windows. La Grande Sauterelle felt quite comfortable dressed as a boy. With the tennis cap pulled down over her eyes, she stared at everybody and commented on the weird people; she turned and whistled when girls walked by.

In the pamphlets from the Automobile Club, the girl had read that the Royal Bank Plaza was made of glass panels dusted with gold. They took the subway to Union Station on Front Street, and as they came out of the station, there they saw the famous building in the light of the setting sun. Its two golden prisms soared into the sky amid the dull grey buildings.

They crossed the street like robots, not looking to see if any cars were coming, and approached the building so they could walk around it and study it from every angle. The light seemed to come from inside. The building looked as bright and warm as honey, and they couldn't help thinking about the gold of the Incas and about the legend of Eldorado. It was as if every dream was still possible. And for Jack, in his heart of hearts, it was as if all the heroes of his past were still heroes.

VII

The Secret Life of the Volkswagen Minibus

To become reconciled with herself.

That was what La Grande Sauterelle wanted, and to do so, she must sleep in the cemetery beside the grave of old Chief Thayendanegea.

At sunset, Jack drove the girl to the cemetery. He acted as if he thought her plan was the most normal thing in the world. He had not voiced the slightest protest when, after only a few hours on the road (they had got no farther than Kitchener), she asked him to leave the 401 again, this time to drive to Brantford, burial place of the famous chief whom the whites called Joseph Brant.

He knew that Joseph Brant had been a great Mohawk warrior, that he had fought beside the English and had remained loyal to the British Crown during the American Revolution. That was all he remembered, but La Grande Sauterelle knew far more than he; she had alluded to the important role of women in the Six

Nations confederacy, of which the Mohawks were part, and she seemed to believe that one way or another, the old chief could help her come to know herself.

Jack pulled up outside the cemetery. The girl took off her boy's outfit, put on a dress and took along her sleeping bag, the cat and a flashlight. The iron gate to the cemetery was closed with a chain and padlock, but they had no trouble jumping the fence. The main path led to a small white chapel with arched windows, around which about thirty graves were scattered among the trees and bushes. It was a very small cemetery. They moved cautiously among the tombstones, deciphering the inscriptions by the light of the flashlight. Right against the wall of the chapel, on the right-hand side, they found the grave of Thayendanegea; it was protected by an iron fence.

"Here it is," the girl whispered.

In the enclosure where the old chief lay there were also the grave of his son Aheyouwehs and, off to one side, that of his wife (her name was not indicated). Not far from the fence, they saw the grave of the Mohawk poet Pauline Johnson. La Grande Sauterelle decided to spread her sleeping bag in the narrow space that separated the burial places of the old chief and the poet. She switched off the flashlight.

"This will be a perfect spot to sleep," she said.

"Aren't you afraid of the cold?" he asked.

"Not in the least."

"I can lend you the long johns if you want."

"That's very kind, but . . ."

"They're thermal," he insisted. "They're guaranteed, even for the Far North."

"Thank you," she said gently. "My sleeping bag's very warm. I could even use it in the snow if I wanted."

The cat had gone, but from time to time they could see his blue eyes gleaming among the tombstones. The moon had risen and a few stars were already glittering in the sky.

"Good night," she said. "Thank you for bringing me here and for not asking questions."

"You're welcome," he said. "Good night!"

He took a few steps and then came back.

"If anything happens, do you know how to get to the campground? You take the road that follows the river and . . ."

"I know," she said.

"Good night!" he said. "Sleep well!"

"You too!"

He hesitated briefly, then he said, "Good night to old chief Thayendanegea!"

"Good night!" the girl murmured, like an echo.

"Good night to his son Aheyouwehs and to his wife who has no name! And good night to Pauline Johnson!"

"Good night!"

"Good night to all those who sleep here!" he said again before he left.

"Good night to you and the old Volks," she replied.

THE CAMPGROUND was on the shore of the Grand River. It was actually a huge park, one section of which had been fitted out for camping, with water, electricity, picnic tables and toilets.

Jack was parked close to the river, and he had no close neighbour. He spent an hour at the picnic table doing nothing but listening to the murmur of insects in the dark, dreaming vague dreams and munching chocolate cookies. Finally the mosquitoes and black flies forced him back inside the minibus. He turned on the radio and listened absently to the nine o'clock news and the weather forecast while studying a road map to see how far it was to the American border. Then he started reading one of La Grande Sauterelle's books, *The Indians of Canada*, but that reminded him that he still didn't have the faintest idea what his next novel would be about, so he closed the book, lowered the bench and lay on the bed with all his clothes on.

The man was very fond of the old Volks.

When he'd bought it, the year he'd won a literary prize, the Volks was already four years old and pitted with rust. He had rebuilt almost the entire underside of the body, using sheets of galvanized metal that he had cut, bent and rivetted in place, then he had repainted the vehicle with antirust paint. The thick metal and the heavy rivets made the minibus look like an armoured truck. Under the new metal, however, the rust continued to do its work, as you could see whenever the Volks drove out of a parking space: it left a fine powdering of rust on the ground.

From old bills he found in the glove compartment when he was cleaning up, Jack learned that the Volks had been purchased in Germany; it had driven around Europe and crossed the Atlantic on a freighter, then it had travelled along the east coast, from the Maritime provinces to southern Florida. In the bottom of the baggage compartment were some shells and coloured stones. The cupboard behind the seat had an odour of cheap perfume, which sometimes drifted into the vehicle at night when it was hot and humid. And here and there, on the walls or inside the doors of the plywood cupboard, were all sorts of graffiti; a mysterious inscription in German, under the sun visor on the driver's side, read: *Die Sprache ist das Haus des Seins*.

Probably on account of its age, the Volks had its peculiar habits. The seat belts, for example: once they were buckled it was very hard to unfasten them, and you had the impression that the Volks was reluctant to let people go. The same with the windshield wipers: they would stop when you turned the button but then all of a sudden, as if they were afraid they'd forgotten something, they would start up again and make one more pass before they stopped for good. But the foremost characteristic of the minibus was that it very much disliked being hurried. Until it was warmed up in the morning it preferred to travel at a reduced speed. It hated, under any circumstances, to be pushed beyond its cruising speed, which was one hundred kilometres an hour, and the impatient driver who exceeded that limit could expect all sorts of protests: the visor would suddenly drop and block his view, or the roof would come undone and threaten to lift off, or suspicious sounds would be heard from the motor or the gears.

The old Volks had travelled 195,000 kilometres in its lifetime, and it wanted respect for its age, its experience and its odd little ways.

THE SUN HAD ALREADY RISEN when Jack awoke with a start. He wanted to get there before the guard arrived, so without taking time to eat or shave he hurried off to the cemetery.

La Grande Sauterelle was sitting in the sun, her back against the white wall of the chapel.

"Did you sleep well?" he asked.

"Very well," she said.

"You weren't cold?"

"No. Just a little, about five in the morning, but then the sun warmed me up."

"Where's the kitten?"

"He went for a walk when I started my exercises . . . Aren't you going to ask if anything special happened?"

"I didn't want to . . . Did anything special happen?"

"Nothing happened at all," she said rather sadly. "I mean, I feel exactly the same as before. There's no difference. Total failure."

"I'm terribly sorry."

"Thank you . . . First of all there's the business about Thayendanegea's wife who . . . I mean, she has no name and I spent part of the night wondering why, and I asked myself all sorts of questions about the old chief — how he treated his wife and all that — and then I wondered why he liked war, why he fought against the French and against the Mohicans from the Hudson River Valley, and finally, when I ran out of questions, I realized I'd lost confidence in him. And that's it."

"So then what did you do?" asked Jack.

"Nothing. I went to sleep," she said, making a funny face.

"Did you dream?"

"Yes. I dreamed about my mother."

She rolled up her sleeping bag and put the flashlight inside.

"Tell me about it, just to see . . ." he suggested.

"I dreamed about things she used to tell me, to put me to sleep. She'd tell me what it was like when she was little. In the fall, she and her parents would leave the river bank where they'd spent the summer fishing and go north for the winter to hunt and trap, like the other families in the tribe. The women prepared the pelts that the hunters brought back to the cabins from their expeditions, and sometimes they'd take part in the hunt. The children were free to do whatever they wanted, and they weren't punished when they made errors in judgement. My mother said that the Indians never suffered from the cold and they never ran out of food. If a snowstorm went on for days and the hunters couldn't bring back fresh meat, they would eat the dried or smoked fish they'd brought from the south, and no one complained. And that's what I dreamed."

"So then you can't say that nothing happened at all," said the man. "As you can see . . ."

"That's true," she said. "Besides, I remembered an observation by another Indian chief. The great Chief Joseph. He said, 'My young people will never work, men who work cannot dream, and wisdom comes to us from dreams.'"

"That's a fine observation," he said. "Is there anything else?"

"No!" she said, laughing. "Shall we go?"

VIII

A Very Quiet Place

"Where are you from?" asked the customs officer.

"Quebec," said Jack.

"Where are you heading?"

"St. Louis, Missouri."

"How long will you be there?"

"I don't know."

The customs officer, who was noting the responses on a form, chewed his pen. It was after four p.m. and there was a long line of cars behind the Volks waiting to cross the border between Windsor and Detroit.

"Vacation or work?" asked the officer.

Jack hesitated.

"I'm looking for my brother," he said.

"Are you? And what do you do for a living?"

"I'm a writer."

The agent jotted something at the bottom of the form.

"Park your truck over there and go to the Immigration Service," he told Jack, handing him the form. "Give this paper to the officer. And take some identification with you. Passport or driver's licence. Understand?"

Jack parked the Volks where the officer had indicated. He suddenly remembered that the cat hadn't been vaccinated, and he asked La Grande Sauterelle to put him in her sweatshirt hood in case the minibus was searched. At the immigration office he was received by a girl with very short hair and a severe expression. He handed her the form and his driver's licence and said, smiling, "I don't know why they sent me here. I don't want to emigrate to the United States!"

The girl looked at him coldly. She studied the papers and started to ask the same questions as the customs officer. Then she inquired, "What do you write?"

"Novels," said Jack.

"What kind of novels?"

It was the standard question, and he'd never been able to come up with a satisfactory answer. How many kinds of novels were there? What category did his belong to? To answer these questions he would have had to be able to state the main subject of his novels . . . And that he could not do, for the simple reason that, for him, writing was not a means of expression or communication but rather a form of exploration. Each of his novels had been written in the following manner: he had placed two characters together in a certain setting and then he had watched them live, intervening as little as possible.

"Love? Adventure?" the girl persisted.

Jack decided in favour of the first, because it included the second.

"Love," he said, looking the girl in the eyes. He was expecting to see something special there, a flash, a sign of complicity or intelligence — a glimmer of some sort. But the girl's eyes were as grey and cold as steel, and her face was like marble.

She asked some questions about Théo. How long had he been in St. Louis? What was his address? What kind of work did he do? Had he become an American citizen? Finally, weary of vague replies, she asked him to stay in the immigration office while she went to inspect the Volkswagen. Through the window, Jack saw that La Grande Sauterelle was walking away from the minibus with the cat in her hood. The grey-eyed girl came back ten minutes later and told him he could go.

"Everything's in order," she said.

"May I ask you a question?" Jack inquired.

"Sure."

He constructed the sentence in his head, then asked, "Was I under suspicion because I'm a writer?"

"No. Because you don't seem to know anything," said the girl.

"Maybe that's why I'm a writer," Jack said jokingly.

"I think you'd better go," she said, and the man had the distinct impression that he shouldn't push the matter.

They stopped at a visitors' bureau on their way into the city, but it was closed.

"What time is it?" asked La Grande Sauterelle.

"Five to five," he said. "What shall we do?"

"It depends whether you want to look for traces of Théo or not."

"I don't really feel like it. This city is grey and dirty. I'm anxious to get to St. Louis. How about you? What would you like to do?"

"If we could find a post office I'd like to mail the book I borrowed in Toronto," she said.

"All right," he said.

"And one other little thing . . . I read somewhere in the literature about Detroit that there's a museum with a Diego Rivera mural, so I'd like to go and have a look at it . . . really, just a quick look. Would you mind terribly? Anyway, the museum closes at five-thirty."

"All right," he said. "But after that we'll get back on the road and make some progress before dark, okay?"

"Okay. Shall we start with the museum?"

"Yes. And we won't look for my brother's trail."

"I promise," she said.

The museum was the Detroit Institute of Arts, and La Grande Sauterelle knew exactly how to get there. They went north on route 75, then west on 94, and they drove along Woodward Avenue to the museum. They bought their tickets, then climbed up to the second floor, racing through a number of galleries on the way, and it was five-fifteen when they arrived, out of breath, in the large gallery that contained the Rivera mural.

The room was nearly ten metres high, and it was lit by the natural light that came in through the glass roof. Rivera's work covered all four walls. In tones dominated by pale green, pale yellow and, above all, grey, it depicted huge industrial machinery with blank-faced workers bustling around it.

The machines, they realized as they studied the different parts of the mural, were those used in the automobile industry. On the north wall, workers were manufacturing motors: they were casting the metal, moulding the cylinder blocks and operating two huge pieces of equipment used to drill the openings for pistons and valves. On the south wall, the workers formed an assembly line, at the left of which was a conveyor belt and, on the right, a giant press that moulded the parts for the body.

All the faces were immutably serious, solemn almost, and their gravity added to the impression of austerity emanating from the drab colours. The overall effect was one of heaviness, sadness and exhaustion.

Just as a guard announced closing time, they spotted, in the very middle of the mural, on the south wall, a small stain of bright red. As they drew nearer they saw it was an automobile coming off the assembly line. The line was set out in such a way that it moved away from the viewer, and the automobile at the other end seemed very small. The tiny red car was the only spot of bright colour in Rivera's immense mural.

Not far from the museum they found a post office where La Grande Sauterelle mailed her parcel. They left the Volks in the parking lot. They were tired and depressed and hungry. They wanted to have a bite to eat and a little walk before they got back on the road.

They bolted some soup and a sandwich in a snack bar. Then they started walking through the neighbourhood.

They crossed a park.

There was nothing special about the park: trees, flowers, benches, a path; some blacks were sitting and drinking beer. It was a quiet spot.

The sun was about to set.

They walked aimlessly. It was only half-past seven, yet the streets were almost deserted.

Jack had no sense of direction. He turned two corners and was totally lost. The girl, on the other hand, could walk for an hour, turning left and right depending on her whim of the moment and always knew exactly where she was.

Sometimes the man had doubts about what she said.

That night, they walked for about an hour, then La Grande Sauterelle declared that they had come full circle.

"Are you sure?" asked Jack.

"Of course," she said. "Look over there: that's the park we just crossed. The post office is just on the other side."

"Oh, yes? Do you think so?"

The girl saw a man making his way along the sidewalk towards them. He was carrying a violin case and a bag of groceries.

She asked him, "Excuse me, sir. Could you tell me where the post office is?"

"Right over there," said the musician, aiming his violin case in the direction the girl had indicated to Jack.

"On the other side of the park?"

"Yes. A few streets beyond it. Five-minute walk or so."

"Thank you."

"Thank you very much," said Jack.

"You don't live around here?" asked the musician.

"No," said the girl.

"We are from Quebec," said Jack.

The musician looked at them for a moment with a sort of fellow feeling, then he said, "Go back to your hotel . . . The sun's gone down and it's getting real dark."

"Why do you say that?" asked the girl.

"This is a rough town. You don't go out on the street after sunset."

They looked at each other, taken aback.

"Go back to your hotel if you want to stay alive!" said the musician abruptly.

They thanked him and very quickly crossed the street. They were about to step onto the path that ran diagonally through the park when a cry made them turn around.

"NO!"

Planted on the sidewalk on the other side of the street, the musician was watching them.

He shouted, "DO YOU WANT TO GET KILLED, YOU FOOLS? DON'T GO *THROUGH* THE PARK! GO *AROUND* IT!!!"

IX

The Saddest Song in the World

La Grand Sauterelle took over the wheel in Detroit and drove the Volks along route 94 for two hours without stopping, then traded places with Jack. He announced that he felt good and that he would drive to Lake Michigan and perhaps even as far as Chicago.

The man had a number of strange little habits. When he drove he was always nibbling on cookies that he took out of a bag he kept between the seat and the door, and from time to time he would talk to the old Volks; he would say all sorts of things such as, for example: "How's everything, pal? Not too tired? Want to stop for a while?"

The man and the girl had a tacit agreement: the one who was not driving had to talk to the other so he wouldn't fall asleep at the wheel.

They talked a little about the Rivera mural. They agreed that the red car was a symbol for happiness and that Rivera had wanted to express something very simple: happiness is rare and getting it requires a lot of trouble, fatigue and effort. The girl said that the same idea was expressed in a song by Georges Brassens, which she started to sing:

> There's nothing a man can count on for sure
> Not his strength nor his weakness nor his heart
> And when he believes that he's opening his arms
> His shadow is that of a cross.

"It's a poem by Aragon," she said. "Do you know it?"

"Of course," he said, without taking his eyes off the grey and dreary highway.

"I like it when he says 'nor his heart,'" she said.

"Me too."

"It might even be the saddest song in the world."

"Could be."

He knew other sad songs and he sang some of them, including "*Un Canadien errant*," and the girl sang two or three as well, until finally they decided to organize a competition that would be called "Contest to Find the Saddest Song in the World."

There was a long silence, then the girl said that the Volks' motor was running well; the valves were a little noisy but everything seemed normal. She had a great affection for the Volks, even though it was old and slow and temperamental. She thought it was just big enough for two. And it had been fixed up so handily, with the retractable roof and the table that could open for making meals, and the seat that could be turned into a double bed when you wanted to sleep; you just had to draw the curtains and you were at home. Like a house . . . The girl had never had a real house. She had been born in a trailer because when her mother married a white man she had lost her house on the reservation at La Romaine; she had been expelled and lost her Indian status. But whites still considered her an Indian, and they had refused to rent or sell a house to the newlyweds. In the end, her parents had bought a trailer.

She told him that she had actually thought about the trailer the night before, because of her father and because of a road sign between Chatham and Windsor that read "Merlin County". The sign had reminded her that, in her father's trailer, there were the thirteen volumes of the *Encyclopédie de la Jeunesse* and that when she was little she had read in one of them a story about Merlin the Sorceror. There was King Arthur and his miraculous sword, Excalibur. And Sir Lancelot of the Lake. There were the knights in search of the Holy Grail. She recalled an illustration on the right-hand page that showed a young and noble knight beside a white horse; he had come to a stop in the middle of the forest, and his face was illuminated by the vision of the Holy Grail; the caption under the illustration read:

Sir Galahad
His strength was as the strength of ten
Because his heart was pure.

From time to time there was another road sign that read "Soft Shoulder". The girl said that was her favourite sign; she didn't like the French expression *accotement mou*, but whenever she saw Soft Shoulder, she thought about all sorts of pleasant things: a soft place to lay one's head, friendship and the warmth of another person. Then she said that she was very comical, with her stories about knights and road signs, and she was probably carrying on like this from fatigue.

She decided to take a little rest on the back seat, with the cat.

To keep from falling asleep while he was driving along route 94, Jack turned on the radio. He listened to the news: the United States was sending military advisers to Central America, unemployment was up, there were floods in Louisiana and a drought in Egypt, Israeli planes were bombing Lebanon, the price of gold had risen, France was conducting nuclear tests in the Pacific, disarmament negotiations were at an impasse. He turned the knob, looking for music, and to his great surprise he suddenly heard a French song, sounding far away and lost in a sea of English words — an old French song that he knew very well; he adjusted the dial until he heard the words very distinctly:

America's road is long
And long is the road of love
When suffering's done, happiness takes its turn
So don't you grieve, my dearest, I'll be home
Wandering's what holds you when you're young
But I'll grow old, my love, so don't you mourn.

America! Every time he heard the word Jack felt something stir in the fog that muddled his brain. (A boat casting off and pulling slowly away from terra firma.) It was an idea wrapped in ancient memories — an idea that he called the "Great Dream of America." He thought that in human history, the discovery of America had been the realization of an old dream. Historians said that the discoverers were looking for spices, gold, a passage to China, but Jack didn't believe a word of it. He maintained that since the beginning of the world, people were unhappy because they could not recover paradise on earth. They had retained the image of an ideal land and they searched for it everywhere. And when they found America, it was their old dream come true, and they would be free and happy. They were going to avoid the errors of the past. They were all going to make a fresh start.

In time, the "Great Dream of America" had been shattered like all other dreams, but from time to time it was revived, like a fire smouldering under the ashes. It had happened during the nineteenth century when people travelled West. And sometimes, travellers crossing America found traces of the old dream scattered here and there, in museums, in grottoes and canyons, in national parks like the ones at Yellowstone and Yosemite, in the deserts and on the beaches like those in California and Oregon.

X

Al Capone, Auguste Renoir and the Nobel Prize

The feeling of sadness that had swept over them in Detroit melted away in the night, somewhere on the road between Lake Erie and Lake Michigan, and they felt relaxed, confident and almost happy despite their fatigue when they reached Chicago about two a.m.

The YMCA was at the corner of Chicago and State streets. This time, the girl disguised herself as a boy before they went in. They were given a room on the fifteenth floor, where they went to bed immediately and slept till noon.

They had breakfast in the cafeteria.

"Do we visit it, yes or no?" asked La Grande Sauterelle.

"What?" said Jack.

"The city of Al Capone," she said. (She pronounced it Al Capo*né*.) "The city of Eliot Ness, of prohibition, of gangsters in black limousines, of bursts of submachinegun fire that shatter the windows in bars and poker dens."

"Why do you say Capo*né*?"

"That's my Italian accent. How do you pronounce it?"

"Capoo-ooo-ooon!"

"That sounds like a lugubrious wind!"

"You're very comical this morning," he said. "And your tennis hat is absolutely irresistible."

"Thank you," she said. "I feel terrific. If you want to get back on the road to St. Louis right away, I'm your man!"

"Aren't there any little stops you want to make?"

"Not one."

"Not even the top of the Sears Tower?"

"Not even! You?"

"Hmm!" he said.

He gave a piece of bacon to the cat, who was on his lap.

The girl guessed, "I know, you're the one who wants to make a little detour . . ."

"Yes," he said. "When I woke up at noon I remembered something: when my brother first left for the States, he used to send letters or postcards, and one day in a postcard from Chicago, he mentioned a painting by Renoir — I think it was a woman with a red hat and lots of flowers — and he said he'd thought about me because I like Renoir so much. He preferred Van Gogh because of the strength of . . . But he said that if I was ever in Chicago . . ."

"It must be at the Art Institute," said the girl, well informed as always.

"We won't stay long," said the man as he drained his cup of coffee. "Just in and out."

IT WAS LATE MAY and the air was soft and warm; Michigan Avenue, animated, broad and opulent with its department stores, restaurants and art galleries, sloped gently down to the Chicago River, the skyscrapers and the Art Institute, which was on the left, on the other side of the bridge.

They asked a guard to show them where the French Impressionists were, and after climbing a staircase they found a gallery devoted entirely to Renoir. Jack spotted the woman in the red hat right away, but first he went around the room, looking at the other pictures, then he went and sat on a bench in front of the painting Théo had told him about.

It showed a young woman sitting on a terrace with a little girl. The painting was entitled *On the Terrace, 1881.* Behind the woman was an iron railing covered with flowering shrubs and then a row of trees through which one could catch a glimpse of a river, some people in a small boat and, in the distance, houses and hills. The little girl wore a white dress and a flowered hat, and her hands were resting on the rim of a basket of fruit that was set on the table. The woman seemed very young; she wore a black dress and a hat of an incredibly bright red; the expression on her face was infinitely gentle, and that gentleness blended with the light that pervaded the entire painting.

Jack looked at the painting without a word. His mouth was open, his gaze fixed and eyes moist. He was utterly still. La Grande Sauterelle stayed with him for a few minutes, then she went to look at the pictures in the surrounding rooms. When she came back he hadn't moved. She told him she'd seen all sorts of interesting things: Cézannes, Seurats and a beautiful painting by an artist she didn't know at all, Gustave Caillebotte, but he did not reply. So she toured the entire floor and came back an hour later, saying she'd seen a stained-glass by Chagall that was superb — the theme was the arts and freedom — and he absolutely had to come and see it. Still motionless on the bench facing the woman in the red hat, he mumbled a couple of indistinct phrases of which the girl understood nothing but the words "light" and "harmony," which she just managed to make out. She went away for the third time and, after visiting all the rooms on the three floors of the building and after seeing everything there was to see, including an exhibition of oriental art and another of prints and drawings, she went to the basement cafeteria and bought two cups of coffee, then came back to the Renoir room. As Jack seemed not to notice her, she decided to stand between him and the painting; she faced him.

"You'll get a sore back," she said softly.

His vision grew blurry, then he fixed his gaze on her.

"Hello," he said. "What time is it?"

"Four o'clock," she said, handing him a cup of coffee.

He had a sip, then took a few steps in the room.

"I'm a bit stiff," he said.

"You've been sitting there for three hours."

"Three hours? What were you doing?"

"Walking around. This is a really beautiful museum."

"Oh, yes!" he said, with a last glance at the Renoir.

She took his hand and led him outside. He was smiling blissfully and she left him alone. She didn't ask a single question. She took him onto Lake Shore Drive because she wanted to see the waterfront before they went back to the YMCA.

Jack felt like eating a pastry or something of the sort, so they stopped at the Holiday Inn.

In the hotel lobby flashes were going off and a group of journalists was crowded around an individual sitting in an easy chair. La Grande Sauterelle went over to see who it was. A reporter was taking notes; she looked over his shoulder and read the name Saul Bellow.

Jack started when she told him the name.

"What? Saul Bellow? Are you sure?"

"Of course I'm sure. Why?"

"He's a famous writer! Don't you know him?"

"No."

"But he won the Nobel Prize! The Nobel Prize for Literature, in 1976!"

"In 1976 I must have been . . . about thirteen," she pointed out.

He was nervously pacing back and forth.

The girl asked, "Do you want to go and talk to the Nobel laureate?"

"I wouldn't dare," he said. "I haven't read any of his books."

"What difference does that make?"

"I can't even remember any titles . . ."

"I've got an idea," she said. "Just call a bookstore and they'll tell you."

He gave her a pleading look that she understood. She went to the telephone. When she came back she handed him a piece of paper on which she had noted two titles: *The Adventures Of Augie March*, 1953, and *Humboldt's Gift*, 1975.

"That's right, I remember!" said Jack.

"Now's your chance . . ." she said.

Saul Bellow had just said, "I've got a plane to catch," and the reporters were moving away. The girl elbowed her way to the front row. Jack hid behind her. A reporter with a tape recorder slung over his shoulder was asking one last question. Sitting in his easy chair, the Nobel laureate formulated a reply, but at the same time, with a sidelong glance, he was peering at the girl's running shoes, jeans and military shirt, and when he got to the tennis cap covering her head he smiled and winked at her. Finally he rose and took his leave of the press.

He had short grey hair and a rather gentle manner.

"I don't think you're a journalist, young lady?" he said in a questioning tone.

"No. But you're supposed to think I'm a boy!" said La Grande Sauterelle with her very pronounced accent.

"Sorry about that!"

"I forgive you because you won the Nobel Prize. I'm a mechanic and my friend here is a writer."

She moved aside and Jack nervously shook Saul Bellow's hand.

"How do you do?" said Jack.

"Nice to meet you," said the winner of the Nobel Prize. "Are you from Quebec?"

"Yes."

"You can speak French if you want: I was born in Montreal."

"What are you doing in Chicago?" asked the girl.

"I happen to live here!" he laughed. "What about you?"

"We're travelling," said Jack.

"Just passing through?"

"Yes. *Oui.*"

"Like your ancestors, Louis Jolliet and Père Jacques Marquette!"

"And Robert Cavelier de La Salle," said the girl.

Everyone started to laugh.

Saul Bellow glanced at his watch.

"What do you think of Chicago?" he asked. "She's been a wicked city in her time, but . . ."

"Wicked?" asked La Grande Sauterelle.

"I mean rough. Now the violence is still here but it's mixed with business and culture. This is the city that gave birth to the *Encyclopaedia Britannica*, Zenith TVs, Wrigley's gum, Quaker Oats and McDonald's hamburgers. But take a walk downtown and there are sculptures and paintings by Picasso and Calder and Chagall . . . Strange city . . . I don't know if I like her or not. But I think she's in my blood."

There was a moment's silence, then the girl said, "We like Chicago very much. She's a beautiful city."

"Where are you going from here?" he asked.

"St. Louis," she said.

"*Je cherche mon frère*," stammered Jack.

"Beg your pardon?"

"I'm looking for my brother."

"He lives there?"

"I don't know."

"Maybe yes, maybe no," said the girl.

The Nobel laureate gave them a curious look, then in a mock-solemn tone he declared, "When you're looking for your brother, you're looking for everybody!"

He translated the sentence himself into hesitant French,

"*Quand vous cherchez votrè, vous cherchez tout le monde!*"

He burst out laughing and they laughed with him, then he walked away, waving goodbye.

XI

Starved Rock

Before they left Chicago, around five p.m., they went to a library because La Grande Sauterelle wanted to "borrow" a book. Jack found a *Petit Robert* dictionary of proper names, and in the entry for Saul Bellow he read the following excerpt from *The Adventures of Augie March*:

> I am a sort of Columbus of those near-at-hand and believe you can come to them in this immediate terra incognita that spreads out in every gaze. I may well be a flop at this line of endeavor. Columbus too thought he was a flop, probably, when they sent him back in chains. Which didn't prove there was no America.

LATER, ON INTERSTATE 80, he recited the quotation to the girl while she was driving.

"It gives you a funny feeling," she said.

"What do you mean?" he asked.

He was sitting in the back seat.

"It's as if Saul Bellow is telling us we're on the right path and that he's wishing us good luck," she said.

He slowly got out of his seat and, approaching her from behind, gave her a kiss on the neck; she started and veered slightly to the right, which landed two wheels on the soft shoulder for a second, then she got the Volks back on the road.

He apologized.

"It doesn't matter," she said. "Maybe I'm a little tired."

"Want me to drive?"

"No, no. We're nearly at the Starved Rock State Park."

He took the navigator's seat and began to study the road maps.

"We're very close," he said. "Twenty kilometres at most."

" It's a very special place," she said. "Do you know the history of the Illinois?"

"No."

"The Illinois don't exist anymore; they're a vanished tribe . . . Do you know the history of the Mississippi?"

"I know about the expedition of Louis Jolliet and Père Marquette."

"Okay," said the girl, "but they stopped at the Arkansas River. The final part of the Mississippi was explored by Robert Cavelier de La Salle. La Salle's lieutenant, Henri de Tonti, built a fort — Fort St. Louis — at the peak of a rock, and that's the rock we'll see at Starved Rock State Park."

For some years, Fort St. Louis had been New France's main trading post in the Mississippi Valley. La Grande Sauterelle knew a number of the figures who had left their mark in the region: Lamothe-Cadillac, Henri de Tonti (known as the man with the iron hand because he had a hook in place of the hand he had lost in a war), Nicolas Perrot, Pierre-Charles Le Sueur, Greysolon du Lhut, Père Louis Hennepin, Pierre Pépin, Radisson and Des

Groseilliers: she knew these people and a number of others, but she was more interested in the fate of a tribe that used to live around the rock: the Illinois.

"The French called them *les Illinois du Rocher*," she said.

"And then they exterminated them, I suppose?" asked Jack. "You called them 'a vanished tribe' . . ."

"No, that's not it. They were exterminated — by other Indians!"

"Ah!" he said.

The girl seemed to guess what he was thinking.

"Were you afraid of another one of my tirades against the whites?"

"Yes," he confessed.

"Well, your heroes can rest easy . . . for the time being, anyway!"

They drove off the Interstate and onto route 178, which took them to Utica; Starved Rock State Park was very close by. They took the cat with them and, because the day was drawing to a close, they began at once to climb the rock, which was forty metres high. Some rudimentary steps had been cut into the south face so that visitors could reach the peak: on the three other sides, the rocky wall was absolutely vertical and it plunged into the Illinois River.

At this late hour, there was no one at the peak. Somewhat winded, they made their way along the edge of the cliff and looked out at the long barges gliding down the river, on their way to the Great Lakes or the Mississippi; they tried to imagine how the rock must have looked in the seventeenth century, when it was surmounted by Fort St. Louis; and then La Grande Sauterelle announced that she was going to tell him the story of Starved Rock.

It was a legend rather than a true story, and it explained both how the Illinois had been exterminated and why the rock was known as Starved Rock, or Rocher de la Famine.

The girl sat on the ground with her back against a big rock.

"In the olden days," she began, "the Illinois lived around the rock. They had been there for a long time and it was their country — I mean, they hadn't just arrived. They led a normal existence and they were happy and unhappy like everybody else. They lived in a region where nature was very rich: there were white pine, elm, maple and oak and a tremendous quantity of wild fruits and grasses of all sorts; they could hunt bison, deer, muskrat, beaver and rabbit, and there were squirrels and a great many birds; the river provided them with fish and fresh water; and on the other side of the river was a very fertile plain where they cultivated corn and squash.

"However, the rock made the other tribes envious because of its favourable location, and despite their peaceful nature, the Illinois were nearly always at war; they were obliged to protect their territory from the Iroquois, who came from the area around New York, and against the Renards, the Sauk, the Pottawotami, the Kikapoo and most of all, the Ottawa, who came from the north and the east.

"When the white explorers, missionaries and settlers began to arrive, the Illinois offered them hospitality and lived in harmony with them. However, the chief of the Ottawa, whose name was Pontiac, had resolved to unite all the tribes of the Midwest in order to rid the land of whites. The Illinois refused to be part of this alliance and, to reap vengeance, Chief Pontiac declared war on them. After a number of fierce, bloody battles, the Illinois, who were about to succumb, outnumbered by their enemies, were reduced to asking for peace. Unfortunately, during the negotiations, Chief Pontiac was murdered.

"The news of Pontiac's death spread like wildfire and a large number of tribes rallied around the Ottawa, intent on wiping out the Illinois. During the ensuing battles, most of the Illinois were killed. All that remained of the tribe was a small number of warriors, women and children, who took refuge at the peak of the rock. They were safe there, for the rock's smooth walls dropped vertically into the river and it could be climbed on only one side, and by just one enemy at a time.

"Instead of storming the rock, the Ottawa and their allies laid siege to it. They positioned themselves around the huge block of stone and waited patiently until thirst and hunger forced the Illinois to leave their refuge. The Illinois stayed at the summit of the rock for three long weeks. When their supplies ran out, they ate the dogs that were up there with them. After that, they ate grass, roots and bark. One day there was nothing left to eat and nothing to drink. They tried to draw water from the river, using a bucket hung from a long rope, but the Ottawa, who were posted at the base of the rock, cut the cord and made off with the bucket.

"Nonetheless, the Illinois refused to surrender to their enemies. Some tried to escape under cover of darkness; the assailants captured and killed them. Others took their own lives by diving off the rock into the river. The rest stayed where they were and died of starvation and thirst. Of all the members of the tribe known as 'the Illinois of the Rock,' there was not a single survivor.

"Later, the place where these tragic events had occurred was called 'Starved Rock' or *'le Rocher de la Famine.'* For many years, all Indians passing through the Illinois River Valley would make a detour to avoid the rock, because it was a place inhabited by death and by the spirits of the tribe that had been exterminated.

"And that's it," said the girl in a tired voice. "That was the story of a vanished tribe, the Illinois of the Rock."

She struggled to her feet, called her cat and climbed back down the stone stairway, holding Jack's hand. The sun had set some time before and the Illinois River looked mauve.

XII

The Old Man Beside the Mississippi

On route 80 not far from Davenport, they were suddenly aware of a strange smell. La Grande Sauterelle, who was in the back writing a letter to her mother, came and sat in front. Jack sniffed the air and looked on either side of the road.

It was a damp, oppressive odour, dense and sludgy, like the smell in a swampy woods, a mixture of water, earth and plants, an aroma of muddy water and old moss.

As they drove up to a bridge, they saw a very broad waterway, its water heavy and yellow; both realized without having to say a word that it was the Mississippi, Father of Waters, the river that divided America in two and joined North and South, the great river of Louis Jolliet and Père Marquette, the sacred river of the Indians, the river of the black slaves and of cotton, of Mark Twain and Faulkner, the river of jazz and the bayous, the mythic, legendary river that people said merged with the soul of America.

On the other side of the bridge, Jack took a road that led to Davenport and, once he had reached the city, he drove the minibus toward the docks; they ended up at a huge lot that contained parking facilities and a disused port authority station.

Before them lay a wharf where a few bums were loafing and an old man was looking out at the river; there was nothing special about him, aside from the fact that his brown, wrinkled skin made him look very old. They got out of the Volks to go and greet the Mississippi. It was hot and humid, and the muddy river waters rolled lazily toward the south. Jack paused, then approached the old man and exchanged a few words with him.

Later, when they were back on the road, he tried to explain something to the girl; it was hard to find the right words and he hesitated.

"Every time I . . . It's the same every time," he said. "Whenever I see an old man on the shore of a river, I have to go and talk to him — I can't help myself."

The road they were on now was no longer route 80, but 61, and it headed not west but due south. This was the road they would follow to St. Louis.

"For a long time, I wondered why I did it," Jack went on. "I didn't understand. I'd see an old man beside the water and every time, something urged me to go and talk to him. Today though, I think I've figured out why."

He said no more; he let the silence go on until finally the girl asked what it was that he had figured out.

"Now that I want to say it, it sounds absolutely ridiculous," he said.

"It doesn't matter," she said.

"Here it is," he said. "What old men are gazing at, when they dream beside the water, is their own death; I'm old enough now to know that. And I talk to them because deep down I have a question or two I'd like to ask them. Questions I've been asking myself for a long time. I'd like them to tell me what it is they've seen on the other side and whether they've discovered what you have to do to get there. And that's it."

XIII

A Wave of Memories

They arrived in St. Louis on the first of June.

It was noon, it was very humid and sultry and they didn't know where to go. How do you set about finding a man in a city of eight hundred thousand? Should they go to the police station? Do research in museums and historical societies? Run an ad on the radio or in the newspapers? They asked themselves these questions and a number of others as they strolled down Fourth Street. They had left the Volks beside the Mississippi, in an outdoor parking lot just a few steps from the Gateway Arch.

Jack and the girl had been captivated at once by the metal arch, whose elegant silhouette, rising 192 metres in the air, cut off a vast portion of the sky above the houses; they had spotted it from far away because it was made of stainless steel and gleamed in the sun.

They walked around for a while in the part of town next to the old Court House and Busch Memorial Stadium, then came back to the parking lot. They had not found answers to their questions, but at least they had reached a decision: as their stay in St. Louis seemed likely to be long and as they must start cutting back on expenses, they would stay in the parking lot rather than take a hotel room or look for a campsite; La Grande Sauterelle undertook to obtain permission from the young man who, working from a booth with a wicket in it, served as the parking lot attendant.

The next day, Jack placed an ad in the city's two leading newspapers, giving a telephone number for Théo to call if he wanted to contact him: the number was that of the parking lot booth. And then they waited to hear from him. Beneath the metal arch, they visited an underground museum devoted to the conquest of the West: the Museum of Westward Expansion. In their different ways, both the man and the girl were crazy about museums and had seen all sorts, but the Museum of Westward Expansion was without a doubt the most fascinating, most amazing one they'd ever seen. In the 1840s, St. Louis had been a meeting place for people who had heard that in the West, on the Pacific coast, the land was vast and fertile; they had sold all their possessions, bought oxen, covered wagons and provisions for six months, then joined a caravan that would cross the desert, ford rivers, scale mountains, brave foul weather, disease and sometimes Indians, until finally, after a five-thousand kilometre journey, they reached the Promised Land. The route taken by these wagon trains was called the Oregon Trail, and one of the starting points was St. Louis; in fact, the metal arch testified to the fact that in the mid-nineteenth century, the city had been the Gateway to the West.

Jack and La Grande Sauterelle spent long hours in the underground museum. Then one day something happened to the man. As he was coming out of the museum, a wave of memories broke over him unexpectedly. The man's memories weren't original; they were even very ordinary, like those of everybody else — a woman who goes off with another man, a crumbling self-image, some lost illusions — but at times they came back so forcefully that he was overwhelmed. That was what happened on the day in question, and he put on his unhappy expression and withdrew into himself. He saw the dark side of everything.

He tried to read a book about the Mississippi that La Grande Sauterelle had "borrowed" from the museum bookstore. It was *Explorers of the Mississippi*, by Timothy Severin. The Spaniard Hernando de Soto was the first white man to see the Mississippi; a bloodthirsty brute, he had come from the south and killed almost all the Indians he encountered along the way. It could be said that Louis Jolliet and Père Marquette had behaved fairly well except that, like everybody in those days, they considered Indians to be inferior beings. Robert Cavelier de La Salle was a great explorer and a great visionary, but his story was a series of murders and betrayals, and he himself had been murdered in Texas, in 1687; his lieutenant, Henri de Tonti, imposed his authority on the Indians by striking them in the face with his famous iron hand.

Violence burst out on every page, and eventually he stopped reading. He spent two days in a state of almost total despondency. Now and then he would walk to the river, where he sat and dreamed. Most of the time he stayed in the Volkswagen and slept.

La Grande Sauterelle spent a lot of time in the parking lot booth. It was just big enough for two people. The young attendant was a student, and they were the same age. When he finished work she would go for a walk with him. He was tall and broad shouldered, he had blond curly hair and a tan. He had studied French in college. Now he was studying business administration at the University of Missouri.

One night she came in very late — it was more like morning — and Jack woke with a start when she shut the door of the Volkswagen.

She took off her clothes.

"Something smells good," he said.

"It's me," she said. "I took a bath and then I put on powder. It's called Spuma di Sciampagna. That's Italian."

"Is it now?" he said with a hint of irony.

Standing in the small space that remained when the seat was transformed into a bed, the girl unfastened her long black braid. He raised the sheet, inviting her to get in beside him. When it was hot he didn't use his sleeping bag; he would open it out and lie on top of it, covering himself with a cotton or a flannel sheet. The girl took off her knife and snuggled up to him.

"You're hot," she said.

"I don't go walking around outside at ungodly hours," he said in a mock-severe tone.

She laughed, and then, in a pleading voice, said, "That's right, give me a lecture."

His answer was a sigh.

"Are you sleepy?" she asked.

"No, not really."

"Well . . ."

"All right," he said. "First of all, a well-brought-up young lady doesn't talk to strange men . . ."

"No?"

"No. She waits to be introduced."

"Is that so? You mean I shouldn't have talked to you when we met in Gaspé?"

"That's different."

"Why?"

"Don't argue!"

His voice became stern.

"Second," he began, "a well-brought-up young lady doesn't go to a strange man's house."

"No?"

"No. Especially not at night!"

"That's true," she said. "What else?"

He pondered for a moment, but couldn't think of anything else to say.

"Lecture me a little more," she pleaded.

"I don't like lecturing," he said. "You're free and you don't belong to me. And I'm falling asleep. I haven't had enough sleep."

She put her arm around his waist.

"What I like most about you," she said, "is your gentleness and your respect for people."

"I'm not really gentle," he said impatiently. "Now you'll have to excuse me. I haven't been feeling well for two days now and I need some sleep."

"Just a minute," she said. "I've got a couple of things to tell you."

"Tomorrow!"

"Right now!" she insisted.

"All right," he said, and turned onto his back.

The girl stroked the hair on his chest.

"I learned some interesting things from Johnny," she said.

"Who?"

"Johnny. The parking lot attendant."

"Don't tell me he knows Théo!"

"No, but he knows a man who met him. A reporter . . ."

"Huh?" said Jack.

He sat up abruptly.

"Now don't get all excited," said the girl. "The reporter didn't *really* meet him, he heard about him."

"How come? What do you mean?"

La Grande Sauterelle got up, heated some water and made herself a cup of Nescafé, then she lay down again, propped on her elbow. The black cat jumped onto the bed and curled up in a ball against her stomach.

"Well," she said, taking a sip. "The other night, Johnny asked me what we were doing in St. Louis and I told him we were looking for Théo, that we'd picked up his trail first in Gaspé and then in Toronto, and that the trail had led to St. Louis. Then he told me he knew a reporter and that if there was one man who could give us any information, it was him, because he was doing research for an article on St. Louis's French background and he'd met a lot of Francophones. And last night, there was a bluegrass concert at the museum and Johnny and I went to it and the reporter was there. He gives talks to the tourists who visit the museum. He's old, about forty-five, but very nice . . ."

"Hmm!" said Jack. "That really is very old. No doubt about it, he's a fossil!"

"I'm sorry," she said. "Anyway, he's older than you. But he's very nice and he speaks French very well. He told me the whole story of St. Louis — how it was founded in 1765 by Pierre Laclède and young Auguste Chouteau, and about the first colonists and the fur traders — and he knows all kinds of interesting things: for instance, he told me Laclède was in love with Chouteau's mother and it's possible he founded St. Louis out of love for her."

"Hmm!" said Jack.

"And he told me about Daniel Boone," she said. "He was one of the first colonists who crossed the Appalachians and settled in the Kentucky forests. He lived in harmony with nature as easily as the Shawnee, the Cherokee and the other tribes of the region. I may be developing a crush on him."

"Hmm!" said Jack. "And what did the reporter have to say about Théo?"

"Oh yes! He said he'd seen his name in a newspaper. Not a St. Louis paper. It was in Independence, a suburb of Kansas City, and the paper was called *The Examiner*. There was an article about Théo. He remembered Théo's name very clearly, because it was written in the French way, with an accent, and also because the article described an incident that reminded him of the first colonists."

"What kind of incident?" asked Jack.

"He didn't remember exactly."

"But he remembered Théo's name!"

"That's what he said."

"That's absolutely ridiculous! It's been twenty years since Théo was here. How could that reporter remember a name twenty years after the fact? It doesn't make sense!"

"You don't understand," said the girl. "I know, the newspaper article's old, twenty years old. But he didn't read it twenty years ago! I mean, really! He said he read the article last spring, in March or something like that. The article turned up when he was doing his research on the Francophones in St. Louis, and he remembered Théo's name because it was a French name, as I already mentioned. That makes sense, doesn't it?"

"Of course," said the man impatiently.

"So what's wrong?"

"I don't know, it's just me. It's my brother . . . It's in my head." With a gesture of impotence, he added, "It's America. You start to read the history of America and there's violence everywhere. It's as if America was built on violence."

The girl offered him her cup of coffee. He drank the last mouthful, then set the cup in the sink. As he raised the curtain he saw a bluish gleam on the horizon, on the other side of the Mississippi. He lay down on the bed, his hands behind his neck. He couldn't get back to sleep. The girl's breathing became regular and deep. An hour later he got up without a sound and went to a McDonald's for breakfast.

XIV

The Captain of the Natchez

They didn't leave for Kansas City right away.

They spent another two days in St. Louis in case Théo should answer the ad they'd placed in the newspapers. And meanwhile, La Grande Sauterelle was doing all she could to bring Jack out of his torpor. She took him for an excursion on the Mississippi in a paddle-wheel steamer.

Their boat was called the *Natchez*. With its two tall smokestacks and its sidewheel, it looked exactly like the steamboats that used to transport passengers and bales of cotton between St. Louis and New Orleans in the 1820s. But this one was a sham, a reproduction built for tourists: that was the first thing they learned after they had boarded the boat along with the other passengers and seated themselves on a wooden bench close to the ship's rail, with hot dogs and coffee. They learned all sorts of things from the loudspeakers that broadcast the captain's voice, and they knew it wasn't a recording, because the captain frequently interrupted his historical reflections to give orders to the sailors or explain the reasons for a manoeuvre.

There was a slight breeze on the Mississippi, and it wasn't too hot, not even in the sun. Jack had to acknowledge that the excursion was enjoyable and instructive.

The captain described how St. Louis had looked during the last century, with its unpaved streets, its storehouses for furs, its shops and boutiques and the candlelit inns where trappers arriving from the West mingled with shopkeepers, soldiers and immigrants from the East or Europe; he described the lively atmosphere around the pier in the early 1840s, while families set on going west to seek their fortunes waited to board a steamer with their wagons, ox teams, barrels, trunks, provisions and their broods of youngsters. They would travel up the Mississippi a few miles, then take the Missouri to the little town of Independence, where the wagon trains formed that, in April, would set out along the Oregon Trail.

When the boat had completed its voyage and returned to the wharf opposite the steel arch, the captain emerged from the wheelhouse and joined the passengers who were heading for the gangway and land. He was a grey-haired man of about fifty, wearing a cap emblazoned with the name of the boat. Having noted that Jack and La Grande Sauterelle were speaking French, he came up to them and said that northwest of St. Louis, in St. Charles, the little town where he had been born and still lived, there were a number of Francophones; his neighbours, in fact, were called Blanchette, and he had learned a few words of French when he played with their children as a boy.

To avoid having to repeat once more that he was looking for his brother and all that, Jack asked him a question — the first one that sprang to his mind — about the date on which the caravans used to set out for the Oregon Trail. Why April rather than May? he asked. The captain replied that since the caravans had to cross the Rockies before the first snowfall in autumn, the people took to the road as soon as the grass was high enough to feed the cattle they brought with them, and that was usually in April.

The captain knew a tremendous amount about the Oregon Trail — the route, the wagons, the climate, the Indians, diseases and accidents — and they listened to him with great interest. Finally Jack gathered his courage and asked the question that was uppermost on his mind. He wanted to know what kind of people had decided, in the early 1840s, to give up everything and travel across most of a continent simply because they had heard that the land was good and life was better on the shores of the Pacific. What sort of people had had the courage to do that?

"Ordinary people," the captain replied.

He took a watch from his jacket pocket and looked at the time, then repeated in French, "*Du monde ordinaire.*"

"Not adventurers?" asked Jack.

"No."

"And not bums?"

"Not at all," said the captain, bringing his hand to his hat in a salute to an elderly lady who stood at the foot of the gangway, holding a poodle and waving a lace handkerchief.

XV

The Deep-Sea Diver's Complex

"Feeling better?" she asked.

"So-so," he said.

"Well then, I think its time for me to play psychologist again . . ."

"Why?"

"Because . . . there are two of us. We're together. We can't live as if we were absolutely separate."

"Mmm, I guess so . . ." he said.

"At least tell me what you're thinking about."

They had been travelling along route 70 for four hours and were almost at Kansas City. The girl was driving. As the road was straight and monotonous, she drove in a very relaxed manner, forearms resting on the wheel.

Jack was studying a map of Kansas City, trying to locate the campgrounds listed in an Automobile Club guide.

"Okay," he said, "I'll tell you a couple of things. At least I'll try . . . First of all, at the age when most people really begin to live, I started to write, and I've been doing it ever since, and during that time life kept going on, as well. There are people who say that writing is a way of living; if you ask me, it's also a way of *not* living. I mean, you shut yourself away inside a book, a story, and don't pay much attention to what's going on around you, and then one fine day the person you love most in the world takes off with someone else you've never even heard of. Second . . ."

He checked something on the map, then folded it and put it back in the glove compartment.

"Second, it's entirely possible that I've never loved anybody in my whole life, It's a sad thing to say, but I think it's true. In fact, I don't think I even love life and I don't think all that much of myself."

"Maybe you love your books?" the girl suggested.

"No."

"Why?"

"They don't change the world," he said peremptorily.

"Do you think they should?" she asked.

"Obviously. Otherwise why go to all the trouble."

He uttered a couple of oaths before resuming his exposition.

"Third," he said, "it's about my brother Théo. That's a little more complicated and I'm not sure I feel like . . ."

"You don't have to," she said.

"I have to talk about it otherwise you'll think I'm a real *zouave*. It's been about twenty years since I've seen my brother, so he's half real and half invented. And if there was another half . . ."

He laughed nervously.

"The third half would be me, I mean the part of me that's forgotten how to live. Do you understand what I'm trying to say?"

"No," she said.

"Neither do I," he laughed, "but it doesn't matter . . . One final thing: my brother Théo and the pioneers. The relationship between them might not be very obvious, especially because I've only remembered some trivial details about him to tell you — a big house, a garden, a river, a snowmobile, that sort of thing. But I'm positive there's a link and it's likely this: my brother Théo, like the pioneers, was *absolutely convinced that he could do whatever he wanted*. And that's just about everything I had to say. Now take the first exit on the right."

The exit came up sooner than he had anticipated. The girl, who was driving in the left lane, flicked on the turn signal and switched to the middle lane. She braked abruptly and, jerking the wheel to the right, slipped between two cars and took the exit with tires squealing.

INDEPENDENCE OVERNITE TRAILER PARK.

As the name indicated, it wasn't a genuine campground, just a parking lot with the most basic facilities: electrical outlets, toilets and showers.

There were no trees. With the sun beating down on the roof of the old Volks and the heat rising from the pavement, it was like being in an oven. On the other hand, they were near the spot where they were supposed to meet the reporter who had read the article about Théo. The meeting was to take place in Independence Square, in the premises occupied by the Jackson County Historical Society on the second floor of the Court House.

Independence Square was lined with shops, houses, restaurants and stores; in the centre a number of sidewalks and staircases, along which public benches were set out, led to an old building surmounted by a steeple: the Court House.

It was three p.m. when Jack and the girl arrived at the Court House. An attendant told them where the historical society was located. They were greeted very amiably by a woman whose grey hair was tinged with blue; she telephoned the reporter, who arrived fifteen minutes later.

The reporter kissed La Grande Sauterelle on both cheeks. He addressed her by her Montagnais name, Pitsémine. He was a tall man with red hair and a heavy moustache in the shape of a circumflex accent. He spoke French very well. His name was Ernest Burke, but in his opinion that was a corruption of "Bourque," the name of his French-speaking ancestors. The woman with the blue-grey hair suggested that everyone sit around a long table, and she asked the secretary to bring refreshments.

The Examiner had not been put on microfilm; it was simply bound in volumes, each of which contained the issues for a three-month period. The article on Théo, said the reporter, was near the end of a volume. So they all began to look through the last pages of each volume, and after a mere half hour's research, La Grande Sauterelle found the article.

She read it aloud. The article said that Théo was being held on suspicion of a break-and-entry committed at the Kansas City Museum of History and Science. The museum guard, an old man of sixty-eight, had been struck on the head with a blunt instrument; he had suffered a concussion and was in critical condition in hospital. The thief had tried to make off with an old map, hand-drawn in 1840 by a Jesuit of French origin, Père Nicolas Point. The map was labelled *Plan de Westport*. It was reproduced at the end of the article.

"Westport was a village around twenty kilometres west of Independence," the journalist explained. "You could say that it's the cradle of Kansas City. How would you say that in French?"

"*Le berceau de Kansas City*," said La Grande Sauterelle. "So the map Théo wanted to make off with was a very important document?"

"Yes and no."

"How's that?"

"It was a reproduction. Apparently the original map is in Montreal, in the archives of a Jesuit college."

"Maybe Théo didn't know that."

"It's possible . . . Was he a historian?"

All eyes turned to Jack.

He was pale, He was rubbing his eyes and he seemed tired.

The girl answered in his place.

"He wasn't really a historian," she said.

"Just a minute," said Jack, raising his hand.

He muttered something incomprehensible, then his voice became steadier.

"You're going too fast," he said. "You're forgetting one very important thing: there's no proof that Théo was guilty. Perhaps he was wrongly accused."

"We can check," said the reporter. "We'd just have to read the court records in *The Examiner*. We'd find out if there was a trial and whether Théo was found guilty."

Jack looked at his watch. He spoke to the woman with blue-grey hair. "What time do you close?"

"Five o'clock," she said.

"It's twenty to," he told the reporter. "Too late to start digging around today."

He got to his feet and thanked everybody.

The reporter accompanied them to the door and walked a short distance outside. He had plenty of things to tell them. He said that every time he crossed Independence Square he just had to shut his eyes and he could see the wagons with the teams of oxen, people on foot or horseback, pack-laden mules, children running in the dust, and he could hear the shouting in the shops and taverns and the sound of hammers and anvils in the blacksmiths', wheelwrights', harnessmakers' and saddlers' shops.

Jack wasn't listening at all, but the man went on to say that some years, immigrants came to Independence in such great numbers there wasn't room for everyone and they had to camp outside the town; and then the glow of the campfires burning in the night would be visible from a distance of several kilometres.

THE NEXT MORNING, Jack refused to get up. More precisely, he got up, drank the orange juice La Grande Sauterelle had prepared for him, then pushed away his bowl of cornflakes and lay down again without saying a word.

"What's wrong?" asked the girl.

He shook his head and, despite the humid heat, wrapped himself in his sleeping bag. After breakfast the girl left a note to say she was going for a walk in Independence Square.

When she returned just before noon, she saw through the window of the Volks that he was still in bed and decided to have lunch at a restaurant. She didn't come back until six o'clock, but he still hadn't got up. So then she gently wakened him. She took his temperature: it was normal.

"You don't have a fever," she said. "In fact it's below normal."

He gave her a wide-eyed, vacant stare.

"Are you hungry?" she asked.

"No."

"You haven't eaten a thing since morning. You have to eat something."

"Why?"

"To stay alive."

He shrugged and curled up in his sleeping bag. About nine o'clock he got up to go to the bathroom and then, without a word, went back to bed for the night.

Next morning it was raining, and La Grande Sauterelle couldn't get a word out of him. He stayed in bed and refused to eat. When she tried to talk to him, he turned his face to the plywood wall that held the medicine cabinet.

She spent the morning at the Court House library and the afternoon hanging around the shops and restaurants. When she came back to the van, the man was completely motionless and did not reply to her questions. She gave the cat some meat, then went back into town in the rain. She took shelter in a large hall where some fifty people were attending an auction sale. She couldn't understand a word the auctioneer was saying, but he was very comical to watch with his little round glasses, sideburns and the strange monotonous chant produced by his metallic-sounding voice as he raised the bids.

She came back to the van late that evening.

The man did not respond to her "*Bonsoir*," but she acted as if everything was normal. She told him how she had spent her day, she talked about Jesse James, whom she'd read about in the library, and about the terrible tuna fish sandwich she'd eaten during the auction sale. When she ran out of things to say she switched on the ceiling light and picked up a book, which she read until she began to fall asleep.

Suddenly, about six in the morning, she was wakened by the slamming of a door. For a moment she tried to get back to sleep, then she straightened up abruptly. The rain had stopped and it was a little cooler.

Wearing jeans, old slippers and a white undershirt, Jack was coming back from the toilet. He made his way unsteadily through the puddles. His hair was dishevelled and his beard heavy.

The girl opened the big sliding door.

"*Bonjour*, Jesse James!" she said with a little bow.

He looked up at her uncertainly. His face was gaunt, and there were circles around his eyes.

"Hi there, Calamity Jane!" he replied.

His voice was hoarse and quavery.

The girl gave him a big grin, but he stepped into the van without looking at her.

"I'm hungry," he said.

"I'm not surprised," she said. "You haven't eaten for three days."

"My legs are like rubber bands."

He sat at the table and started to fix some orange juice while La Grande Sauterelle set up the Coleman stove, hooked up the big blue cylinder of gas and heated water for coffee.

He squeezed the oranges. His hands were shaking and . . .

"Watch out!" said the girl. "You're getting orange juice all over my book!"

There was a book on the table, open to a page with the story of Jesse James and his brother Frank. A spurt of orange juice had landed right on the photograph on the right-hand page; Jack looked and saw that it was none other than Jesse James, the famous outlaw.

Jean-Louis Rieupeyrout, *Histoire du Far-West*, Tchou, 1967, p. 603.

"This is a library book," said the girl.

"Have you 'borrowed' it?"

"No, but I'll have to if you keep spraying it with orange juice."

"I'm really terribly sorry."

The man didn't look sorry. He was even beginning to feel quite good. He fixed himself a huge glass of orange juice, a bowl of cornflakes with a banana, two eggs with bacon, three slices of toast with raspberry jam and two cups of black coffee.

"Do you know what was wrong with me for the past three days?" he asked La Grande Sauterelle.

"What? Yellow fever?" she said ironically.

"No."

"Bubonic plague?"

"No."

"I give up. What?"

"I had deep-sea diver's complex," he said.

"What's that?" she asked, looking at him to see if he was serious.

He appeared to be serious.

"I'll explain," he said, "but not till you've told me what this business of Jesse James and his brother Frank is all about."

"What business about Jesse James and . . ."

"Don't play innocent," he broke in. "You left your book on the table, open precisely at the page that has the story of the two brothers, Frank and Jesse James."

"Sheer coincidence," she said.

"It wouldn't by any chance be a way of telling me something about my brother?"

"Such as what, for instance?"

"For instance, the idea that even if you love your brother very much that doesn't stop him from being a bandit."

"It never crossed my mind."

She appeared to be as serious as he had been when he told her about his deep-sea diver's complex. There was no way of knowing if she was telling the truth.

"In any case," he said, "I've been thinking a lot about that business of the stolen document, and I came to the conclusion that Théo was a Quebec nationalist. Maybe even a member of the FLQ. He thought the map was an original document, and he wanted to get it back from the Americans and bring it home."

He watched the girl to see what she was thinking, but her expression was still serious and impenetrable. In her black eyes there might have been a little gleam like the one in the eyes of mother hens, but he wasn't sure.

"So tell me about the deep-sea diver's complex: what is it exactly?" she asked.

"Well, it's not all that easy to explain," he said, "but I'll try."

He began to speak slowly, searching for his words, elbows on the table, head in his hands.

"The deep-sea diver's complex," he said, "is . . . It's a pathological state in which a person withdraws into himself when he's faced with problems that seem insurmountable. But in fact the person doesn't really know what's going on, and his behaviour is . . . instinctive. He senses that he absolutely has to protect himself, so he withdraws into the diving suit: first he pulls on the rubber suit that looks like the costume on the character in the Michelin tire ads, then the bronze helmet that's as round as a ball and has three little windows covered with a mesh, and finally he puts on his heavy lead soles, otherwise . . ."

"I know, I know," said the girl. "And then?"

"Then he slowly goes down the ship's ladder into the water. He's safe inside the diving suit. The water doesn't seem too cold. He goes down deeper and deeper and the light dwindles. The half light is very pleasant, and it's also very comforting to know that there's someone on the surface of the water watching over you and operating the pump to give you air. You feel safe and you keep descending. Finally you come to the bottom of the water: it's calm and you feel very comfortable. There's just a tiny bit of light.

You hardly feel like moving. You're in a new world. You're really very comfortable. You'd like to stay there forever . . . And that's it. That's the deep-sea diver's complex."

La Grande Sauterelle poured herself a cup of coffee.

"Now I understand something," she said.

"What do you understand?" he asked, somewhat anxious.

"When you came back from the bathroom a while ago, I was watching you walk through the puddles . . ."

"Yes. And?"

"I thought you were having trouble walking and I was wondering why. Now I understand."

"Yes?"

"You'd forgotten to take off your big lead soles!"

XVI

Chop Suey

Shortly before noon, the girl came back from Independence Square with a package that contained a contact breaker, a condenser, four Bosch spark plugs and three litres of motor oil.

She took a groundsheet from her knapsack and spread it under the rear of the Volkswagen because she wanted to check the valves; she thought they were knocking a little, but she wasn't sure. Taking with her the tool kit from the Volks, she lay on the groundsheet and removed the caps that were on either side of the engine. Using a feeler gauge, she checked the play of each valve, going from one side of the engine to the other, and she was pleased to note that no adjustment was necessary.

"Everything's fine," she told the man.

It was at least thirty degrees Celsius on the paved surface of the trailer park, and the last thing she felt like doing was a valve adjustment. On the other hand, she didn't mind giving the engine a little tune-up and even an oil change. She had donned her old pair of shorts and a paint-smeared shirt whose tails were knotted over her bosom. In the nearest trailer, a man was watching her from the window.

She started by unscrewing the spark plugs and then, because they were carbonized, she replaced them with new ones, after she had adjusted the gap between the electrodes. Then she took off the distributor cap.

"Would you bring me my timing light?" she asked Jack. "I'll be needing it in a minute. It's in my big bag. At the bottom. Between two sweaters, probably."

She removed the rotor and saw at once that the contact breaker had a dark blue tinge, so she replaced the breaker as well as the condenser.

"It wasn't in your bag but I found it, anyway," he said.

He set the lamp on the asphalt beside the girl, and she saw that he'd brought an ordinary flashlight.

"What I need," she said without losing her calm, "is a special lamp to regulate the timing. A *stroboscopic* lamp. Do you understand what I mean?"

"Yes, but . . ."

" . . . but you can't imagine me owning one, is that it?"

"That's it," he confessed. "I keep forgetting you're a mechanic. I'm sorry."

He went back to look for the lamp and, as he passed the neighbour's trailer, shot a black look at the man who was gazing out the window at him, smiling.

The girl plugged in the lamp and asked Jack to start the engine. She let it warm up. Jack looked over his shoulder as she shone the flashing beam of light on the timing marks that needed aligning. Once this task had been accomplished, she slid under the vehicle again and drained the motor oil, using the cat's emergency dish. She also checked the oil in the gearbox and the differential.

"That's all I can do," she said, after she had changed the oil in the engine. "I haven't got the tools for the brakes and the lube job. We'll have to go to the garage."

"Of course," said the man. "I don't know how to thank you."

"That's easy," she said. "Fix me something to eat while I take a shower. I'm ravenous."

She was sweating and covered with oil stains. He made her a chicken salad with all sorts of fruit and vegetables: the table was set and everything ready when she came back from the shower, with her hair pulled up and wrapped in a towel, and wearing her white nightgown, though it was the middle of the afternoon.

After their meal she asked if the cat had eaten anything.

"I haven't seen him," said the man.

"No? Was he here last night?"

"But . . . I thought he was with you!"

"So did I!"

She reflected for a moment.

"He must be out in the field," she said.

What the girl called "the field" was just a vacant lot with some clumps of grass behind the trailer park. The cat often wandered off there. It was obvious he wasn't especially fond of asphalt.

"He was born in the country," said the girl. "His parents came from the country and his grandparents, too."

The cat had a full lineage of country ancestors, which accounted for his fondness for long walks in the grass. There was no cause for alarm, but the girl still couldn't resist an urge to go out in the field for a look. She took off her nightgown, pulled on jeans and a T-shirt, got out of the minibus and walked over to the fence; she called the cat softly but he didn't come; she put two fingers in her mouth and whistled: that was no more successful.

Jack joined her. They climbed the fence and walked together in the field; the cat wasn't there. They began to investigate the neighbouring streets; they peered at front stoops and verandas and, if there was nobody around, they inspected lanes and back yards, but in vain. Then they walked aimlessly, going farther and farther from the trailer park. In the end they weren't really looking, because they were positive the cat had come back during their absence.

But the cat wasn't there when they returned to the Volks.

Nine p.m. and still he wasn't back.

Suddenly they were very worried. He had gone away and hadn't been able to find his way home. Or someone had picked him up. Or else he'd been chased by a dog. Or he had followed another cat, perhaps even a lady cat — but no, he was far too young. How old was he exactly? Four or five months. Maybe six. He was really very young.

The girl was in a very bad way.

She felt guilty. She reproached herself for having abandoned the cat in an asphalt trailer park. That wasn't very smart. She should have taken him with her. By force if necessary. She gave him too much freedom. He was too young to know what was good for him. He was still a baby.

Jack told her she had no reason to feel guilty. The person who was really responsible was himself, because he had been so withdrawn that he'd forgotten the cat for days on end. In any event, he was sure the cat would come back.

There had been a great many cats in his life. One summer he had lived in a cottage with two cats, each of whom had given birth to five or six kittens. As a result the cottage had been completely overrun with cats. All of which meant that the cats had frequently wandered off, but they had always come back, and he even remembered a little black-and-white kitten about the same age as the girl's, who had gone away for a week. And then one fine day he'd come back.

Cats have a really incredible sense of direction.

True, said La Grande Sauterelle, but there's the question of territory. As long as cats are on their own territory they manage fine. But when they have no territory?

That night they had trouble sleeping.

They woke up several times because they thought they'd heard meowing.

In the morning, the cat wasn't there.

While they were preparing breakfast in the minibus, they discussed what they would do. First, they would go to the SPCA; they'd look up the address in the phone book and walk there, if it wasn't too far, or take the bus; obviously they'd have to leave the Volks where it was, because the cat might come back at any time. After that, they'd revisit all the neighbouring streets, but this time they would ask the children if they'd seen a little black cat. And perhaps they'd put a notice on the neighbourhood telephone poles.

Jack had taken a shower and was in the washroom shaving when he heard a loud exclamation.

He ran out of the washroom, half of his face covered with white lather.

The cat was home!

La Grande Sauterelle was holding him in her arms and dancing on the asphalt. She was laughing like a loony. A number of people had come out of their trailers and were watching the scene.

"He must be starving!" said Jack.

"You're right," said the girl. "What am I thinking about?"

She brought the cat to the Volks, set him on the table and poured him a big bowl of milk.

The cat sniffed it, but refused to drink.

"That's funny. He doesn't want the milk," she said.

"Hold on," said the man. "I'll give him some ground beef. There isn't a cat in the world that can resist a nice raw hamburger."

He took some meat from the fridge and set it on the table.

The cat refused to eat it. He was purring, but he wasn't eating.

"The meat looks fine to me," said the man. "I don't understand. Maybe he's been hurt . . ."

He examined the cat, but saw no wounds.

The girl said, “Maybe he’s sick . . .”

She touched the cat’s muzzle: it was cool and damp as usual. The cat was in fine fettle.

“It’s simple,” she concluded. “He isn’t hungry and that’s all there is to it.”

“You’re right,” said Jack. “He managed perfectly well on his own. He found something to eat.”

“Maybe a mouse,” said the girl.

“Or a bird,” said the man.

“A drumstick!”

“Shepherd’s pie!”

“Chop suey!”

XVII

The Middle of America

It was very hot in Kansas City, and after they had walked in the sun for just two minutes they were soaked in sweat. Rather than go to Independence Square and do research in the old newspapers at the Jackson County Historical Society, the man stayed in the minibus, leafing through books.

He didn't really feel like reading; he would put a book on his lap and turn the pages or simply stroke it with his fingertips.

There were books in every nook and cranny of the Volkswagen. To the books the man had packed when he left Quebec City had been added those he had bought or the ones the girl had "borrowed" along the way. There were books in the compartment behind the driver's seat; in the glove compartment where the cat slept; behind and under the passenger seat; on the second shelf in the medicine cabinet; in the compartment for saucepans and other kitchen utensils; at the back of the little cupboard where they hung their rain gear; and on the shelf overhanging the back seat. No matter where you were in the minibus, there was always a book within reach.

"I wish I were at the seaside," said the man.

The girl gave him a long look. She had just come in and was sitting in the passenger seat. Taking care not to waken the cat, whom they'd christened Chop Suey, she took the big map of the United States from the glove compartment.

"Look," she said, unfolding the map. "Come here and see something."

He set his book on the table and came over to her.

"Look —" she pointed to Kansas City "— there's where we are. Almost in the middle of America!"

"Still," he said, "I'd like to be by the ocean. I miss the ocean."

"Which one?" asked the girl.

"What?" he asked.

"Atlantic or Pacific? Which do you prefer? Where the sun rises or where it sets?"

She undid her braid, took a brush from the wash stand and began to untangle her hair.

The man reflected for a moment.

"At my age, a sea with a setting sun would be most appropriate," he said. "But you, at your age . . ."

"When do we set out on the Oregon Trail?" she asked abruptly.

"You don't want us to go our separate ways?" said the man by way of response.

"No," she said.

"Why?"

She got the leatherette stool, handed the man her hairbrush, and sat with her back to him.

"Because I feel attached to the old Volkswagen," she said.

The man began by brushing her hair lightly, using short strokes, as he had often seen her do.

"The old Volks could fall apart anytime," he said.

"We'll see," said the girl.

"Your hair is soft. It's as black as a stove, but I've never seen hair so soft."

"Thank you. When do we leave?"

"Do you really think Théo took the Oregon Trail?" asked the man.

"Yes, I do," she said.

"Have you done any more research in *The Examiner*?"

"No, but I saw the reporter again. He gave me a book."

"Oh, yes? How come?"

He had finished untangling the girl's long hair, and now he could brush it with long strokes, over and under.

"Don't you think it's normal?" she asked.

He made no reply.

She turned to him.

"You may be right," she said. "Now that you mention it, I remember he had a weird look on his face."

"Oh, yes?"

"His eyes in particular. I remember very clearly. His eyes were dark and every now and then there was a sort of flash . . . and in the light of those flashes you could see, as if it was at the very back of his eyes, you could see all sorts of things like daggers and swords and rifles and snakes and tigers and crocodiles and rhinoceroses and dinosaurs and dragons and . . ."

"Okay! I get it!" said the man.

When he had finished brushing the girl's hair and redoing her braid, she showed him the book the reporter had given her. She had already started to read it. It was *The Oregon Trail Revisited*, by Gregory M. Franzwa, and the title reminded Jack of something. He had the impression that he'd seen it somewhere, but where? And suddenly he remembered: the police file in Toronto! It was one of the books Théo had in his belongings! He opened his mouth to tell the girl, but she was grinning at him and he saw at once that she had got the point before him and that he was late, as usual. Then to make up for it, he announced, "We're going to leave as soon as possible."

"There's a lot to do," said the girl.

"That's true," he said. "We have to go to the garage to see about the brakes and the lube job. Find out some things about the conquest of the West. Learn how to live. Learn how to love. Buy oranges and food for Chop Suey."

"And do a laundry," she said. "We're out of clean clothes."

THEY HAD BEEN in the waiting room for an hour, absorbed in *Popular Mechanics, Car and Driver* and *Track and Traffic*, when the foreman came and said the mechanic wanted to see them; he showed them to the repair shop.

The mechanic was waiting for them under the Volkswagen, which was kept at the proper height by means of a hydraulic lift. Blond and blue-eyed, solidly built, he appeared to be about fifty. The black cat was perched on his shoulder.

"I found this in the Volkswagen," he said, handing the cat to the girl.

His voice was soft and he spoke French to her with a slight accent that betrayed his German origin.

"It's an odd sort of cat," he said. "He's got no fear of noise and he wants to watch everything I'm doing. What's his name?"

"Chop Suey," said the girl.

"I like cats a lot . . . Your tune-up was just about perfect. I just slowed down the motor a few rpm: that'll save you a little gas."

"Thank you," she said.

Jack walked over and began to peer at the underside of the Volkswagen.

"How's the Volks?" he asked.

"Depends where you intend to take her," said the mechanic.

Holding the inspection lamp in his left hand, he aimed the beam at the transverse rod that connected the two front wheels.

"Have a look here," he said.

He took a wrench from his overalls pocket and tapped the metal part a few times. Scraps of rusty metal came away and fell to the ground.

"It's rusted," he said. "Not completely, but it's half rusted. Now have a look here."

He moved the lamp toward the back of the vehicle and this time shone it on the chassis, between the two wheels.

"Same thing here," he said, striking it with his wrench. "You see? The chassis's half rusted."

"Is it serious?" asked Jack.

"That depends!"

"And how are the brakes?" asked the girl.

"As a matter of fact that's one of the things I wanted to show you," said the mechanic.

He turned the lamp to light the inside of a wheel. Jack and the girl approached.

"Look at this piece," he said, tapping a plate-shaped part inside which the brake linings were attached. "That's the backing plate. I don't know how you say it in French. This part's supposed to be very rigid, but the rust has weakened it so much that if I took off the wheel and unfastened the springs, the brake linings and the rest, I could easily twist the piece with my fingers."

The man had huge hands, and Jack looked away when he made a gesture as if he were twisting an imaginary backing plate between his fingers.

"When you apply the brakes, friction on the brake linings makes the backing plate heat up. But if it's weakened by rust, the heat can twist it and . . ."

"How much for new plates?" asked Jack.

The mechanic switched off his lamp and turned toward the counter where the clerk responsible for parts was standing.

"Peter!" he called. "How much is a backing plate for this '71 bus?"

"Around thirty-five dollars each," the clerk replied. "Want me to check?"

"No. But are you sure they're in stock?"

"Quite sure, yes."

The mechanic explained, "It'd cost you seventy dollars for the two and about fifty for labour."

"That's a lot," said Jack. "Is it absolutely necessary to change the plates?"

"Depends where you're going," said the mechanic.

Jack hesitated.

"We're travelling the Oregon Trail," he said.

The mechanic looked pensively at each of them in turn.

"You're going to follow the Oregon Trail?"

"Yes," said Jack.

"You're going to cross the desert and the Rockies?"

" Yes . . ."

"In the old Volks?"

"All right," said Jack, "I get it. Put in new backing plates and if you notice any other defective parts, replace them, too."

An hour and a half later, they were driving west along route 70.

"The motor's running well," said Jack. "Can you hear it?"

"Yes, it's very smooth," said the girl.

"And the brakes are solid. No vibrations. Shall I do a test? A panic stop?"

"Not now," she said. "There's a car right behind us."

The man looked in the rearview mirror.

"You're right," he acknowledged.

"I'd say the old Volks is in tip-top shape," she said.

He took a chocolate cookie from the bag that he kept beside the seat.

"And what about you? How are you?" he asked with his mouth full.

"Very well."

"But I mean, are you happy?"

"I've everything I need," she said.

He gave her time to explain herself and at length she said, "When we're on the road I'm very happy."

XVIII

The Oregon Trail

They didn't stay long on route 70. Once they arrived at Topeka, Kansas, they headed northwest toward the Big Blue River, one of the first waterways the 1840 emigrants had had to cross, and from there they drove back onto Interstate 80.

Through Nebraska, route 80 closely followed the Oregon Trail, in some places joining it.

All the information they needed could be found in *The Oregon Trail Revisited*. Not only did the book tell them the location of the old trail and how to get there, but it also provided data on each of the historic sites, even quoting passages from diaries the emigrants had kept during their journey.

But Jack and the girl liked the book for another reason: the author's fatherly attitude. For instance, when he said, "Follow such-and-such a route as far as an old barn, take the dirt road, cross a railway track, turn left and drive to the stream, then leave your vehicle and walk a hundred and fifty paces through the grass in a southerly direction, and at that point take a good look at the ruts in the field there: that's the Oregon Trail . . ." When he gave these very detailed instructions, the author would also add that you must be careful at the level crossing because the signals were faulty, or he might advise you to wear boots in the fields because of the rattlesnakes.

The Volkswagen was travelling along route 80. Jack was driving and the girl was reading the book they were in love with. Needless to say they weren't following all the author's instructions; they preferred to stay on the Interstate in order to arrive sooner at the places where there was some chance of finding Théo's trail.

"It wasn't easy to cross the Big Blue," said the girl, holding the book on her lap.

"Oh, no?" he said.

"After the spring rains, the river was broad and deep and the current was very swift, so it was necessary to build rafts."

"But . . . wouldn't the wagons float? I mean, weren't the bottoms of the wagons tarred so they'd float?"

"Yes, but they were overloaded. It's incredible what people brought: besides their food and clothes and weapons and ploughing implements there were big cast-iron stoves, solid oak desks and all sorts of old furniture. Family heirlooms!"

Jack shook his head in disbelief.

"The furniture had to be unloaded and everything put on the rafts," said the girl. "It took several trips . . ."

"Was there a cable attached on either side of the river?"

"Of course."

"And the cattle?" he asked.

"No problem," she said. "The horses were taken across first; the oxen and cows swam across after. Not a single animal was lost."

"That's good. So now everybody's in good shape and we start

off again?"

"Right. There's no time to lose if you want to reach the Rockies before the first snowfall in October. The travellers head northwest, toward the Platte River, and follow along its south shore for a great distance. Along the way, the landscape is transformed. At first, when the caravan left Independence, it was hilly, and with the grass waving on the prairie it was like being on a ship. Now there are fewer trees and hardly any green, just the occasional bush. The landscape is more arid and it's hot. By midafternoon it's really very hot. There are terrible storms almost every day. You get soaked to the bone."

"Aren't the canvas coverings waterproof?"

"They are," said the girl. "But most of the time you're on foot. Walking alongside the wagons."

"Why?"

"The wagons have no springs. Inside, you get badly jolted, so it's more comfortable to walk. And anyway, the oxen are very slow."

"When you're soaked to the bone you're anxious to stop and camp for the night," observed the man.

"That's up to the wagon master to decide. When he sees the sun sinking below the horizon, he gives the signal to stop, and the wagons are arranged in a circle and fastened together. The oxen are unhitched and taken outside the circle, with the horses and the other animals. The children are sent out to gather wood or buffalo chips."

"Buffalo chips? That must stink to high heaven!"

"Oh no, they burn very well and they don't smell at all . . . The men bring out the camp stoves and pitch the tents. The women cook chunks of meat that the hunters have brought back. After they've eaten, the children play nearby, the young people sin
dance to a fiddle or a harmonica while the grown-
the schedule of guard duty for the night and a

ties for the next day's leg. Bedtime is early, between nine and ten o'clock, because the wake-up call is at four a.m."

"What time is it now?" asked the man.

"You're the one with the watch," said the girl softly.

"So I am."

It was five in the afternoon. On Interstate 80 the sun was blinding now. Jack pulled down the sun visor. He was tired of driving, but he didn't want to keep the girl from reading *The Oregon Trail Revisited.*

"Where's the next campground?" he asked.

"At North Platte," she said. "A half hour's drive. Shall I take over?"

"No, it's all right."

"There's a Buffalo Bill museum," she said, and plunged back into her book.

La Grande Sauterelle was addicted to books. She loved books and words. One day she had thrown a tantrum because someone had said: "One picture is worth a thousand words." She had "borrowed" a magazine, taken a pair of scissors and cut out the letters needed to compose the following sentence, which she taped to the Volkswagen's dashboard: ONE WORD IS WORTH A THOUSAND PICTURES.

Her attitude toward books was very special. The most astonishing thing Jack had ever heard was something La Grande Sauterelle said about books one night when they were in St. Louis and were having trouble sleeping because the damp heat from the Old Mississippi was seeping into the Volkswagen. Jack had been depressed that night and he couldn't recall her exact words, but they were something like:

"You shouldn't judge books one by one. I mean, you mustn't see them as independent objects. A book is never complete in itself; to understand it you must put it in relation to other books, not just books by the same author, but also books written by other people. What we think is a book most of the time is only part of another, vaster book that a number of authors have collaborated on without knowing it. That's all I have to say about books and now I'm going to try to sleep. Good night."

JAM PACKED with tourists and utterly bare of trees, the North Platte campground wasn't very pleasant. They grabbed a bite to eat, then went at once to the Buffalo Bill museum.

William F. Cody had been nicknamed Buffalo Bill in 1867, when the Kansas Pacific Railroad hired him to supply fresh meat for its employees; in discharging his duties he had killed a dozen buffalo a day for eighteen months.

"That must add up to five or six thousand buffalo," said the girl.

Her face was hard again and her eyes shone, and Jack saw at once that Buffalo Bill, like his brother's other heroes and his brother himself, was about to come under fire. This time, anticipating her, he himself denounced the buffalo hunter's alleged heroic deeds: he had "killed his first Indian at the age of twelve"; he had become a scout for the despicable General Custer; he had emerged victorious from a duel with Yellow Hand, one of the greatest chiefs of the Cheyenne, and finally he had organized a sort of travelling circus, the Wild West Show, which had been presented in a number of European countries.

The man's tactic assuaged La Grande Sauterelle's wrath and even prompted her to say that not everything Buffalo Bill had done was bad. She recalled that he had been one of the best riders for the Pony Express, the postal service that recruited young men for high-speed mail delivery between Missouri and California; once, when the Indians had set fire to the relay post where he was to have been replaced by another rider with a fresh mount, he had travelled 515 kilometres without a break. She added that toward the end of his life, he had a ranch in Wyoming where he raised buffalo.

"Maybe old Buffalo Bill realized that the buffalo were a vanishing species," she said as they were leaving the museum.

"Perhaps he's even responsible for the fact that there are still buffalo in America," said Jack.

"You don't have to go *that* far," said the girl.

GENERALLY, of the two it was Jack who had more trouble sleeping; he would get up several times every night to eat cookies and reflect on all sorts of things. But that night, at the campground in North Platte, Nebraska, it was the girl who couldn't get to sleep. She twisted and turned, grumbling, and three or four times she kneed Jack in the back.

In the middle of the night she started to mutter some English words in her sleep, words he had heard a number of times before but hadn't understood, and this time he recognized an exclamation he'd seen in one of the books she was reading on the Indians. "White men, big shitters!"

As she was becoming more and more agitated, he touched her shoulder to waken her.

"Huh?" she said.

"You're having a nightmare," said the man.

"Oh . . . yes . . . the buffalo."

She sat up in bed and began to talk about the buffalo. At first her words weren't too coherent, but Jack listened patiently.

"There's a distant hum," she said. "You're on the plain, on the shore of a river, and you're fixing your lunch when all of a sudden you hear a hum, a muffled sound that gets louder. The first thing that occurs to you is that there's a storm brewing . . . You glance anxiously at the sky, but it's blue and there's not a sign of a cloud on the horizon. But the muffled sound is still getting louder . . . You begin to understand that it's coming from the other end of the plain, so you leave your meal and climb a hill and try to see what's going on. First you see a big cloud of dust that reminds you of a sand storm in the desert, like you see in the movies, then you can make out some black dots, many, many black dots, all moving; the black dots gradually get bigger and you can see that it's an enormous herd of buffalo. There are so many that the entire plain can't contain them all. They're running away from something: a grass fire or Indian hunters. The buffalo gallop across the plain and as they pass your hill, their heavy hooves pounding the earth, it's like an earthquake."

The girl recalled that there were almost sixty million buffalo before the arrival of the white man. In those days the Plains Indians hunted only for subsistence, and the hunt was accompanied by ritual ceremonies.

She did not approve of all their methods, in particular the one that consisted of leading a herd to a high cliff from which the animals would hurl themselves and break their bones. But, in general, she thought that the Indians hunted buffalo in an honourable manner. Then, too, while the white man often killed the buffalo for its fur or its tongue, the Indians used every part of the animal.

"The buffalo provided the Indians with everything they needed," said the girl, becoming more animated. "That's why the extermination of the buffalo meant the disappearance of the Plains Indians."

She told how the Indians used buffalo hides to make tents, clothing, blankets and canoes; the horns and hooves for glue, knives, spoons and drinking cups; the muscles, tendons and hair for braided straps and belts; the bones for sled runners; the gastric juices and blood to prepare medicines. The list was endless, and as the girl talked, Jack was more and more convinced that if there was a Plains Indian, just in front of the hill that gave a view of the herd, killing a buffalo with an arrow or a well-aimed bullet behind the shoulder, and if the squaws were arriving to cut up the carcass, soon all that would be left of the great beast would be a little dried blood in the grass and a few tufts of hair.

The girl gulped down a glass of milk and two cookies, then went back to bed. But instead of falling asleep again, she launched into a violent outburst against all the whites who had turned buffalo hunter for financial reasons, like Buffalo Bill or the employees of the fur-trading companies, or for sport, like the rich people who came out from New York or Washington on special trains and, without even stepping outside, unloaded their rifles into herds that beaters had pushed along the railway line; her most unflattering epithets were reserved for the Grand Duke Alexis of Russia, son of Czar Alexander II, who had come to hunt buffalo, complete with his retinue and his cases of champagne, in 1872.

Slowly she calmed down. Jack was sitting across from her, legs folded under him, back resting against the plywood wall, saying nothing. She apologized for having kept him up so long. She helped him get back into bed, then she lit a candle and, in her softest voice, read him the Sioux Prayer for the Return of the Buffalo.

SIOUX PRAYER FOR THE RETURN
OF THE BUFFALO (1889)
Father, have pity on us;
We weep for we are thirsty,
All has vanished.
We have nothing to eat;
Father, we are wretched.
We are very unhappy.
The buffalo are no more,
They have all disappeared.
Have pity on us, Father;
We dance as thou hast commanded
Because we follow thy will.
Though it causes us pain,
We dance and dance.
Have pity
Father, help us;
We are close to thee in the shadows;

Hear us and help us,
Send the white men away,
Bring back the buffalo,
We are poor and feeble,
Alone, we can do nothing;
Help us to be what we once were
Happy hunters of buffalo.

XIX

They Died With Their Dreams

They got up late.

La Grande Sauterelle was in an excellent mood. She took the wheel and the man sat in the navigator's seat. He glanced at the route they would follow along Interstate 80, then immersed himself in their favourite book, *The Oregon Trail Revisited*.

The girl turned on the radio. It was playing western songs, and she started to hum the tunes she knew. One of the songs was very old. It had been composed by Jimmie Rodgers. Entitled "Hobo Bill's Last Ride," it told the story of Bill, a sick and solitary wanderer who had gone to sleep in a freight car one cold, rainy night as the train was charging through the darkness. The last words went:

It was early in the morning when they raised the hobo's head
The smile still lingered on his face but Hobo Bill was dead.

There was no mother's longing to soothe his weary soul,
For he was just a railroad bum who died out in the cold.

With the nostalgic sound of the train whistle and Jimmie Rodgers' nasal voice, the song was worthy of inclusion in the Contest to Find the Saddest Song in the World.

She switched off the radio and asked Jack how things were going in the book.

"Not too badly," he said, "except for the dust . . ."

"The emigrants are biting the dust?"

"They've never swallowed so much dust in their lives. They've pulled handkerchiefs over their noses and the wagons are travelling side by side rather than single file, but the plain is getting drier and drier, so the oxen and wagons are stirring up clouds of dust. And they're out of fresh water."

"You haven't seen a stream or anything?"

"There was a sort of pond," said Jack, "but the water was poisoned."

"Who told you that? Did you see a sign with a skull and crossbones?"

"Hardly!"

Jack shook his head, laughing.

"Of course not," he said. "There's no need for a sign. The rotten smell was enough . . . The guide said that drinking it would mean dysentery or cholera or something of the sort. The water had been poisoned."

"By the Indians?"

"No. A herd of buffalo. The Indians wouldn't do such a thing, would they?"

She reflected briefly. "Well . . . no, not in the early forties."

Then she asked, "What do you mean, you have a guide? Not just a wagon master but a guide, too? A real guide?"

"Of course."

"That's a very well-organized expedition!" she exclaimed.

"And what's your guide's name? Jim Bridger? Kit Carson?"

"They picked someone who spoke French so he could communicate with the Indians."

"French . . . Frémont? Bonneville?"

"A very *special* guide," said the man.

"I see . . . His name isn't Théo, by any chance?"

"Can you give me a good reason why he couldn't be called Théo?"

"No, not really," she said. "Anyway, how are things going with the Indians?"

"So far we've met Kansas and Cheyenne. The Kansas wanted tobacco and blankets. Théo told them, all right, but in return he wanted buffalo meat. The trade was carried out and everything went well. But it wasn't so simple with the Cheyenne. They wanted horses. They said that the caravans frightened the buffalo and they needed horses to hunt them."

"Makes sense to me."

"That's what the guide said, but he didn't agree about the horses. He'd rather give them anything else, even rifles. He wanted to keep the horses for the Sioux. He said they'd soon be in Sioux territory and the Sioux were the cleverest and most demanding of all the Plains Indians. They'd *have* to give them horses. If they didn't trade them, the Sioux would steal them. In fact they were even capable of stealing the horses from one caravan and selling them to the next!"

"Your guide obviously knows a lot about the Indians."

"He knows Indians and he knows the area like the back of his hand. But that's not all. The guide doesn't just do his work: he also helps out the wagon master."

"How?" asked the girl.

"The wagon master's a little bit *zouave*," said the man. "Whenever he has to make a decision, he hesitates. He says it's because his head's full of fog. Do you understand what I'm getting at?"

"Seems pretty obvious. He's *special*, too."

"That's right. In the end, it's Théo who decides when we stop, when we start up again, where we ford a river, how we fix a broken axle, where we have the best chance of killing a bison or an antelope, how we interpret signs along the trail and the Indians' smoke signals and all the rest. Look, he's just galloped by on his horse. Did you see? He was heading for the wagons at the rear and he waved to us as he passed. Now and then the guide checks on things at the end of the convoy: that's where they keep the cows and horses they'll be taking to Oregon, to the Willamette Valley, where they're going to farm the land and raise livestock. The problem with cows is, they always want to wander off and graze. But the horses, they follow the wagons and don't give us any trouble, though you still have to keep an eye on them because of the Indians and also because they might break a leg if they fall in a gopher hole. There are people on horseback whose job it is to keep an eye on the livestock, but the guide would rather check himself, to see that they're doing their job and don't have any problems."

Jack broke off for a moment. He wasn't used to talking so much. When he'd got his breath back he continued.

"It's late June. Since we left Independence, Missouri, we've travelled between thirty and forty kilometres per day; we haven't had any trouble, aside from the rivers to cross, the heat, dust, storms and mosquitoes. The guide knows the terrain will soon be getting rougher and that there are problems ahead, so he takes some time to talk with the emigrants; he explains what's in store and he encourages everyone — men, women and children. He knows the emigrants aren't heroes. They're ordinary people. They were farmers, artisans, teachers and missionaries back in Michigan, Kentucky, Indiana, Ohio, Illinois, Missouri. They're not rich, but they had enough money to buy a covered wagon and oxen and all the supplies they needed for the journey. They're not adventurers. What they're looking for isn't adventure, it's . . . In fact, they don't know exactly. They've heard there are vast fertile lands out west and they've decided to go there, that's all. They think they'll find a better life out there, on the Pacific coast. What they're looking for, basically, is happiness."

There was a long silence. Jack had gone back to reading their favourite book, stroking the cat who was purring in his lap, when suddenly he raised his head and gazed out, perplexed, at the countryside.

"Hey," he said. "Are we on route 26?"

"No, we're on 80," said the girl quite calmly.

"No we *aren't*! I just saw a sign that read 26 WEST. Didn't you see it?"

"No."

"So we're on the wrong road," he said.

"I'm sorry, I wasn't paying attention. I really thought we were still on 80."

"It's my fault. I was the navigator. I should have been doing my job instead of telling you all those stories."

"No, no, they were very interesting."

"You're just saying that."

She winked at him.

"Just a sec, let me have a look at the maps," he said.

Riffling through the literature they'd been given at the Nebraska border, he took out a state map to see where La Grande Sauterelle might have made the mistake that had taken them off highway 80 and onto 26.

It was in the town of Ogallala. That was the only place where the two roads met. From all indications that was where the mistake had been made.

However, there was something strange about the girl's attitude: instead of slowing down, she was driving the Volks at one hundred kilometres an hour; and she was whistling "*Un Canadien errant.*"

He took out the map again but this time he studied it carefully in the light of the information provided in *The Oregon Trail Revisited*. He saw then that the Platte River split into two branches, north and south, and that the Oregon Trail ran along the northern branch. At the same time he saw that from Ogallala, the road that followed the Oregon Trail was not route 80 but 26: the girl had turned right and got on the proper road without saying a word.

"This is the right road," he said. "I was acting like a . . ."

He couldn't find the appropriate word.

"Like a *zouave*?" she suggested.

"Just about."

"Do you feel like a total idiot?"

"Yes."

"You've plumbed the depths of ignominy?"

"That's right."

She started to laugh, while he managed a kind of nervous snicker.

To atone for his absentmindedness as navigator and to hide his confusion, he went back to studying the maps. He announced that they would arrive shortly at a place that was frequently referred to in the emigrants' diaries.

"It's called Ash Hollow," he said. "And there's a campground just outside. But I guess you already knew that . . ."

"I vaguely remember. What kind of ash is it named for?"

"The tree. The guide's just told the emigrants that their troubles are about to begin. And he was quite right. The terrain has been rising gradually, and now the emigrants are on a high, arid plateau. They have to go down a slope that's so steep that they must lock the wagon wheels by fastening them to the body with chains; they make the wagons glide along as slowly as possible by holding them back with cables or even with a winch, but if the cables break, the wagons will go hurtling downhill at a tremendous rate and smash to smithereens when they land in the valley!"

"I hope the cables hold and everybody gets to the bottom of

the hill safe and sound!" said the girl.

"Thank you," said Jack. "Ash Valley is the first shady place they've been in after two months' travelling. And there's also a wonderful fresh-water spring."

"Sounds to me like a good place for a rest," she said.

"We're there," he said.

WITH THE EXCEPTION of five or six government employees busy emptying wastebaskets into a garbage truck or mowing the high grass at the edge of the property, the Ash Hollow campground was deserted. It was a primitive site, with neither electricity nor running water, and the only conveniences were what were commonly known as pit toilets; however, a fountain with a tap in the middle of the campground provided drinking water.

La Grande Sauterelle took a bar of soap and headed for the fountain. She took off her clothes, letting them drop in the short grass, and then, wearing only the leather thong that held her knife, she sponged herself with cold water and soaped her body. She shouted to the man to bring her a towel. The government employees interrupted their work and, scythes in the air, began to watch.

Jack brought her the beach towel, the big one with a lion, parrots and an orange sun on it.

"Thank you," she said.

"I fed the cat," he said.

"You're sweet."

She was drying her hair with the big towel. He jerked his head in the direction of the men who were watching her.

"I saw them," she said.

"But did you see their boots?"

"Of course, they're the first thing I noticed."

"That means there are rattlesnakes, right?"

"You think so?"

She wrapped herself in the towel.

"Out west everybody wears knee-high boots," said Jack. "Maybe you shouldn't go around barefoot."

The girl put on a dress and her running shoes. They took along the cat, as usual, and a thermos of cold water and a bag of cookies, then set off on foot for the top of the hill that the emigrants had descended with such difficulty.

Its name was Windlass Hill, and there was a winding path paved in asphalt that one could climb, with benches to rest on. At the top they could see the ruts left by the emigrants' wagon wheels: hollowed into the rock, eroded by rain, they were surprisingly deep and of a yellow, almost golden colour, like paper discoloured by the sun.

They stood there in silence. They felt like intruders. Out of place. (An old house where elderly people speak in undertones and communicate by secret gestures.)

On their way down, they took a detour to look at an old cemetery, and as they were drawing near they saw a tombstone that had been placed under glass; the epitaph read:

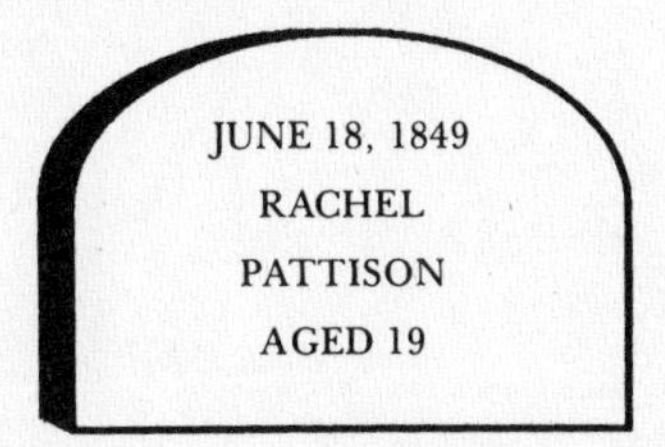

Her name was Rachel. She was nineteen years old and she was dead. Probably of cholera. That's what it said in *The Oregon Trail Revisited*. It also said that thirty thousand emigrants had died along the Oregon Trail and that this number represented one-tenth of the people who had tried their luck. About these thirty thousand, the book said: "They didn't make it." These emigrants — men and women, old and young people and children — had not reached their destination. They had died *en route*, with their dreams. They had died in all sorts of ways: from cholera or dysentery; drowned crossing a river in spate; struck by lightning; killed by Indians; mortally wounded when handling a gun; dead of fatigue, of exhaustion, of sunstroke; devoured by grizzly bears; young children fallen from a wagon crushed to death by the wheels.

For one reason or another they hadn't made it and now their bleached bones lay somewhere along the trail. They had been given a tombstone with an inscription, or a pile of stones with a cross, or they had been buried in an unmarked grave.

But sometimes the graves were desecrated by Indians or wolves. To avoid such profanation, the emigrants would occasionally bury their dead in the middle of the trail, ahead of the caravan, and all the wagons would drive over the grave, one after another, until the wheels caused all trace of the burial to disappear.

XX

The Bull Rider's Wife

She was big and blonde, with long hair and green eyes; she must have been six feet tall.

Her shoulders were broad.

She had a warm, open face, and she provided information to tourists from a mobile home located on a dirt road that led to Chimney Rock.

Chimney Rock was a rocky formation that did resemble a chimney. Some emigrants used to say that it looked like an inverted funnel, but to most of them it suggested a factory chimney or the chimney of a house destroyed by fire. This is what it looked like:

It stood one hundred and fifty metres high and could be seen from far away on the prairie. It served as a reference point. When emigrants spotted the long narrow stone chimney in the distance, they knew that they must soon brave the Rocky Mountains. In fact, on a clear day they could make out the first foothills of the Rockies, the Laramie Mountains, on the horizon.

All day long, La Grande Sauterelle had a premonition that something was about to happen. She didn't know exactly what, but they should be prepared for something important. When they arrived at the mobile home, the tall woman greeted them Texas-style.

"Howdy!" she said, and cordially shook their hands; they felt like old friends.

"How do you do?" they replied in unison.

The woman shot Jack a look of particular interest.

"We've met before, haven't we?" she asked.

"Yes. No!" he said.

He was very excited. Her face was like Melina Mercouri's, a face as round as the full moon, and it was lit by the warmth of her green eyes. She was looking at him as if she recognized someone in him or through him. She didn't know a word of French. He tried to tell her they were from Quebec and all that, but his English was even more infantile than usual, and finally La Grande Sauterelle took his arm as she explained to the woman that they were going to take a look at Chimney Rock and would be back shortly.

"We'll be back in a few minutes," she said, with her amazing accent.

"Sure," said the woman. "Take your time."

The girl drove to the end of the dirt road, where they spent a moment gazing at the rocky column; there was a fence around it, with a notice: visitors who entered the area to get a closer look at the chimney did so at their own risk, because there were rattlesnakes.

"You know," said the girl, "when I said I had a premonition . . ."

"Yes?"

"Well, I was making that up: it wasn't a premonition at all."

"No?"

"No. In fact it was something I've known for a while now. Since Kansas City, to be precise. And I didn't tell you about it."

"That doesn't seem very clear to me," said the man.

"Let me explain," she said. "Remember the journalist I met in Independence, outside Kansas City? Well, just before we left he told me something amazing. He said that if you and I decided to take the Oregon Trail, we had to stop at Chimney Rock and talk with the woman in charge of tourist information. He told me she was a bull rider's wife, that she was very special and that if Théo had passed by and he was the kind of man we imagine he is, the woman would remember him."

"That really is amazing! Twenty years later?"

"Not necessarily twenty years. It could be that Théo spent some time in jail after that business at the museum. Let's say the old guard had died, for instance. Anyway, that's what the journalist said."

"Why didn't you tell me about it?"

"You weren't in any shape . . . The deep-sea diver's complex, remember?"

"Yes," said Jack. "I understand."

He took off his sunglasses, blew on the lenses and wiped them with his T-shirt. Then he asked, "Did you see the chimney? The top part looks as if it's been broken."

"It's made of clay and sandstone," said the girl. "The wind and rain make it crumble a little every day. Apparently pieces of rock come loose now and then and fall to the prairie."

"It makes me think of a big broken phallus," said the man.

They got out of the Volkswagen to walk a little. The black cat got out, too, slid under the fence and walked along a winding path that led to the base of the rocky column.

"I hope he won't be eaten by a rattlesnake," said the girl. "Poor little kitty!"

"He's getting bigger now," said the man. "He can't sleep in the glove compartment anymore, have you noticed?"

"No."

"You know," he said, "I think I've changed, too. What you said about my brother didn't affect me the way it would have before. I mean, it affected me, but it didn't destroy me."

"Is that true?"

"No," he sighed. "It isn't true, but I feel as if . . . I don't know . . . Maybe it's coming very slowly."

"Did you see the way the woman looked at you?" she asked.

"Yes, it felt odd. It was as if she recognized me and was trying . . . But I suppose she just recognized some of Théo's features."

"But didn't you say that you and Théo were very different?"

"Yes, he's taller and his hair is black, not brown, and sometimes he has a beard. But there's still a certain family resemblance."

"So the journalist was right?"

The man did not reply. The only way to find out was to go and see the bull rider's wife again. The girl called her cat and they went back to the Volks.

"Promise me one thing," said the man. "Don't leave me alone with her. When she looks at me with those big green eyes and her beautiful round face all full of light I don't know what to do: my legs turn to rubber and I feel as if I won't be able to get a word out."

The black cat came scurrying up and they drove back to the mobile home. They were greeted as warmly as before. Jack said an entire sentence in English, and it was obvious that he'd constructed it in his head in advance.

"You were looking at me and suddenly I got very excited . . ."

"Oh? Is that so?" asked the woman, with her big smile.

"Yes. Maybe it was because you're so big . . . I mean, tall, and beautiful, but maybe it was because I had a *special feeling*."

"A *special feeling*?" she repeated.

"Yes, madam. The feeling that you recognized me," he said, stumbling over the terrible word "recognized."

"I *did* recognize you."

"Thank you! I'm very happy!"

"So we have met before," she concluded.

"Yes, but it wasn't me," said Jack. "It was my brother Théo."

"Théo?"

She repeated the name several times. Her gaze was lost in the distance. Then suddenly she said, "Oh, yes . . . oh, yes!"

She remembered. It was a long time ago, but she remembered

very clearly. A bright light spread across her face as the memories returned. She said that Théo was a little rough around the edges maybe, but when she talked about him, there was such warmth in her voice and so much light on her face, that it was as if Jack's brother had been absolved, washed clean of all the accusations and all the suspicions of which he had been the object since their journey began.

The woman was silent, and as Jack didn't seem to know what to say, La Grande Sauterelle intervened. "So your husband is a bull rider?" she asked.

"Yes, my dear," said the woman. "He's in Denver and next week he'll be in Cheyenne. He's always travelling to catch a rodeo. Sometimes he goes as far as Calgary. But when he's not too far, he drops in to give me a hand with the rattlesnakes."

Like all rodeo cowboys, her husband didn't receive a salary or any travelling expenses, and he even had to pay his own registration fees. He wasn't paid a cent unless he won something in a rodeo. That was why he occasionally came to Chimney Rock, where he got rid of the rattlesnakes that infested the area around the stone chimney.

The woman told them a couple of things about rattlesnakes. First of all, they don't bite people just like that, for the fun of it. They bite in self-defence if someone inadvertently steps on them while they're warming themselves in the sun or sleeping in a rock crevice. And if you get bitten, the best thing to do is put a chunk of ice on the bite to slow down the blood circulation, and go and see a doctor without getting all worked up.

The main thing to avoid, if you don't want a tonguelashing from the doctor, is enlarging the bite with a hunting knife and sucking the venom and spitting it out, as they do in Westerns; doctors find that the poison harms the system enough without their being required, in addition, to repair the damage a hunting knife causes to nerves, veins and muscles.

La Grande Sauterelle asked the woman what her husband did

to get rid of rattlesnakes.

"How do you kill a rattlesnake?" she asked. "With a gun?"

"With a spade," said the woman. "You just chop their heads off."

The girl grimaced and changed the subject.

"And Théo," she asked, "how was he?"

"Just fine," said the woman.

"In good shape?"

"Terrific shape!"

"How long . . ." (Her voice broke, she coughed and looked furtively at Jack.) "How long did he spend here?"

"A few days, honey."

"And where was he going when he decided to leave?"

"He was heading west, but . . ."

The woman had the impression that Théo was running away from something. In addition, he wasn't sure if he was going to Oregon or California. Across the Rockies, on the Oregon Trail, there was a fork: the road on the left went to California, the one on the right to Oregon. And Théo still hadn't decided which way to go . . . The junction was in Idaho, by the Snake River, near a place called Fort Hall.

When they expressed a wish to leave, the bull rider's wife held out her arms and embraced them. They stayed in her arms for several minutes, happy as children to be enfolded in the woman's marvellous warmth.

On the dirt road they had to take to get back to 26, they turned around for a last look at Chimney Rock. Later, leafing through her books because she vaguely remembered a sentence that she'd read somewhere, the girl found the following passage in a short story by Carson McCullers: "His own life seemed so solitary, a fragile column supporting nothing amidst the wreckage of the years."

It was in a story called "The Sojourner."

XXI

Sheriff Waterman

An hour's drive brought them to Scott's Bluff.

It was an impressive cliff that, from a distance, resembled a fortress, with towers and parapets; at the summit, visitors had a fine view of the Platte River valley and of Mitchell's Pass, which the emigrants took on their way to the Rockies. However, Jack and the girl were more interested in the museum at the foot of the cliff.

In the museum lobby a register lay open on a lectern. Jack signed his name and address. La Grande Sauterelle put down her name as Pitsémine. Then they went to the reception desk and asked to see the old registers.

The person at the information counter was a very young freckle-faced redhead, with her hair in two short braids that stuck out sideways like Pippi Longstocking.

She asked if they had authorization from the National Park Service.

"We don't need that," said La Grande Sauterelle.

"No?" asked the young girl.

"No. This man here is Sheriff Waterman," she said lowering her voice.

The young girl gave them a conspiratorial smile that revealed a mouthful of braces.

"Top secret?" she whispered.

La Grande Sauterelle nodded.

Jack stepped to one side and pretended to be looking at a brochure on the history of Scott's Bluff. The girls were talking amid muffled laughter.

"I don't see any badge on his shirt," said the young girl.

"It's *invisible*," whispered La Grande Sauterelle. "They make them invisible now, for security reasons. Understand? In the old days, a badge made you a *cible* for everybody. A *cible* . . . How do you say that?"

"A target?"

"Yes!"

The young girl opened a filing cabinet, took out a stack of old registers and set them on the counter. She asked if the man Sheriff Waterman was looking for was a "dangerous outlaw."

"Very dangerous," said La Grande Sauterelle.

"A killer?"

"Ssh!"

"SSH-H-H!"

La Grande Sauterelle opened the first register, and Jack came up to look over her shoulder. Even though the registers only went from May to September, it was a big job to examine the list of names. The girl looked at the left-hand page and the man the one on the right. They checked all the registers, but Théo's name was not there.

Disappointed and tired, they decided to go outside.

They asked the young girl to tell them where the ruts were. Scott's Bluff was renowned for the ruts left by the emigrants' wagons. In Mitchell's Pass, where the trail became very narrow, the ruts left in the crumbly soil were sometimes a metre deep. The young girl came out of the museum with them and pointed to an abandoned wagon on the prairie. From there, they could walk in the ruts for two or three kilometres.

"Have a nice day!" she said as she left them.

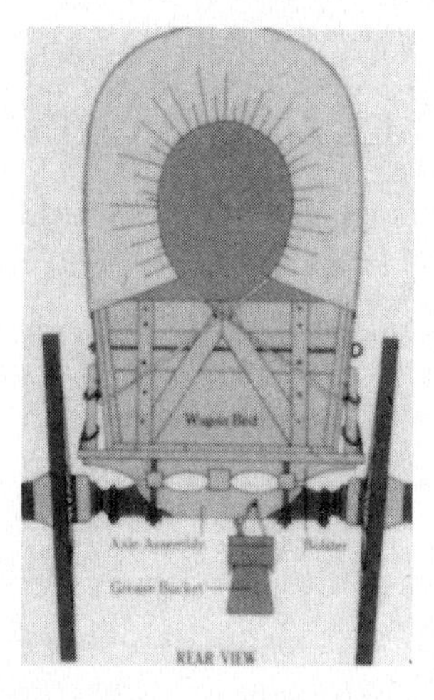

They were pleased to find that the wagon was not a reproduction, but a genuine "prairie schooner," as the emigrants called them. Made of hardwood, it seemed both sturdy and light. It even had a certain elegance. And from the back, it looked really odd, with its angled wheels somewhat like the legs of an old cowboy, and the canvas cover that reminded you of an old woman's bonnet.

They began to walk in the ruts that started at the wagon and continued toward the mountains. After a few minutes they could no longer hear any traffic noise from route 26. It was hot, but there was a little wind. It was a beautiful day. Just three or four clouds very high in the sky.

The man and the girl walked side by side and almost in silence. When they had something to say they spoke in an undertone. As if they were in a church, a cemetery, a sacred place. The ruts, very deep at first, became less spectacular as they went on; after they'd walked for a half hour, the ruts were hardly visible because the ground was hard.

Jack stopped for a moment.

"This is like Théo's trail," he said. "It's something that almost doesn't exist."

"That's true," said the girl. "A strange postcard, a police file, an article in an old newspaper . . ."

". . . and a trail of light across a woman's face."

XXII

The Gatling Gun

"Farewell, Nebraska! Farewell, vast prairies!" the girl cried out as they drove into Wyoming.

Jack asked if they were far from Fort Hall.

"Far enough," she said. "Anyway, it isn't our next stop . . ."

"It isn't?" he asked.

"No. I have to pay a little visit to Fort Laramie."

"But . . . that's an army fort! I thought you hated the military!"

La Grande Sauterelle had declared her loathing of the military several times. She said that of all the armed forces, the group she hated most was the American cavalry. She harboured a special hatred for the American cavalry and for the Seventh Regiment in particular; the Seventh Regiment of the American cavalry was unquestionably the military group that she detested most.

Her eyes would become as black as the stove and they would flash sparks when she talked about Generals Sherman, Custer and Sheridan.

"That's true," she admitted, "but Fort Laramie used to be a trading post. It belonged to the American Fur Company. And it was named after a French trapper, Jacques Laramée, who set up camp in the area in 1818. Besides, in those days all that territory and maybe even the entire American West was flooded with French Canadians who worked as *coureurs de bois*, trappers and guides. They lived with Indian women and many had Indian blood themselves."

She had another reason for stopping at Fort Laramie: in 1854, soldiers at the fort had massacred some Indians who had stolen a cow from an emigrant. Jack paid no attention to this last remark. It was not until a half hour later that he became aware of his error. Each of them was visiting the various rooms in the fort, which had been turned into a museum, when he heard a sort of howl. Like a tremendous cry of despair.

The cry came from the room he was about to visit. He had not immediately recognized La Grande Sauterelle's voice, but suddenly the cry was followed by a familiar exclamation:

"White men, big shitters!"

He rushed into the room.

Red with anger, the girl was pointing to a machine gun. It was a Gatling, a sort of ancestor of the machine gun, with a fixed breech and a number of tubes bracketed together that acted as a barrel and followed a rotary motion.

Five or six people, including a very dignified old lady escorted by two little girls, had drawn closer, trying to understand what was going on. La Grande Sauterelle stood facing the machine gun, fists on her hips and legs apart. She was raging.

"WHAT THE HELL IS THAT?" she exclaimed.

A ranger came forward and broke the circle the people were forming around her. He was a young blond man with little round glasses and a narrow beard along his jawline. He looked very gentle. The girl was crying and shouting and swearing, half in

English, half in French.

"*ESPÈCE DE ZOUAVE!*"

"Beg your pardon?" said the young man.

"YOU SHOOT INDIANS WITH THAT TABARNAK DE MACHINE GUN?"

He looked at the Gatling, but didn't seem to understand.

"Shoot Indians?" he repeated.

"YES STUPID! YOU SEE THIS MACHINE GUN?"

"Yes . . ."

"I WANT TO KNOW IF IT WAS USED TO SHOOT INDIANS! UNDERSTAND?"

"Oh! I see your point."

The two little girls huddled close to the old lady. Everyone held his breath.

"Well, I don't think so," the ranger replied at length.

"WHAT DO YOU MEAN, YOU DON'T THINK SO?" La Grande Sauterelle howled, at the peak of exasperation.

"Please come this way," he said.

The ranger took La Grande Sauterelle to the other end of the room. The tourists followed them, chatting as if it were a guided tour. The old lady asked Jack if "the young girl" was an Indian, and he replied that he had no idea, he'd never seen her before in his life. The ranger took a key from his pocket and unlocked a glass display case and removed a black leather notebook. It was the fort commandant's diary.

Before a silent audience, the ranger carefully turned the pages of the notebook, then began to read an excerpt. The commandant had recorded there a despatch he had sent to the authorities in Washington to complain because the Gatling constantly jammed with black powder from the ammunition, which rendered it totally useless.

As the ranger read, La Grande Sauterelle's face lit up; there was the beginning of a smile at the corners of her mouth and, finally, she started to laugh and the tourists did the same. There was some applause.

The girl vigorously shook the young ranger's hand. She even gave him a couple of friendly pats on the back and declared in her inimitable accent, "This machine gun — I like it very much!"

The storm had blown over.

It was lunchtime, and they munched sandwiches before getting back on the road. La Grande Sauterelle poured some milk for the cat. Jack was driving. The girl said little and seemed very calm. However, that afternoon there was a sudden storm. She told him what had happened at Sand Creek.

"In November 1864," she said, "a Cheyenne chief, Black Kettle, agrees to make peace with the white men and he brings his people and a small group of Arapaho to Sand Creek. That's a little stream seventy kilometres from Fort Lyon, Colorado. At dawn on November 29 a group of six to seven hundred mounted servicemen, who have left the fort during the night and drunk whiskey to warm up, attack the Indian campsite. They are led by Colonel Chivington, who gives the following order: 'Kill them and scalp them all, young and old.' There are five hundred Indians, most of them women and children. Chief Black Kettle hoists an American flag that was given him by President Lincoln. Seeing that the soldiers are pursuing their attack, he raises a white flag, as well. But Chivington's soldiers continue to fire, and they fire at everyone. They fire at women and children. They fire rifles, pistols and cannon. About forty women take refuge in a cave. As a gesture of peace they send out a six-year-old girl with a white flag, but as soon as they see the little girl the soldiers fire at her; then they flush out the women, killing and scalping them. They catch children and smash their skulls against tree trunks. There is a pregnant woman: they kill her, disembowel her and lay the foetus on the ground beside her. When the massacre is over a hundred women and children have been killed, and twenty-five men.

The bodies have been scalped and some of them cut to pieces. Chief Black Kettle has managed to escape and his wife is still alive, though nine bullets were fired at her. And that's what happened at Sand Creek."

La Grande Sauterelle made an effort to calm down again.

She had spoken with a sort of controlled violence. She had an excellent memory and she remembered dates and figures.

The storm had passed and Jack breathed again. He looked straight ahead without saying a word. The road was gradually becoming steeper. The Rockies were very close.

They stopped to eat around six o'clock. Afterwards there was another storm, briefer this time. The girl talked about Washita.

"With seven hundred men," she said, "during the night General Custer surrounds a village of Cheyenne who are camping on the shore of the Washita River. It is November 1868. At dawn, Custer's men, who form the Seventh Regiment of the U.S. Cavalry, launch an attack to the sound of bugles. They come from all sides at once, and in a few minutes they massacre a hundred men, women and children. Among the dead are Chief Black Kettle and his wife. This time, their luck ran out, though old Black Kettle had realized that the Indians were no match for the whites in battle and he'd done his best to persuade the other chiefs that they must seek peace. And that's it."

La Grande Sauterelle got up and went for a walk. They were camping in a park that belonged to the town of Douglas. It was the first time they had used a municipal park; there were no showers, but the park was huge, with plenty of greenery, and admission was free.

Jack took advantage of the calm to make coffee and read a chapter of *The Oregon Trail Revisited*. He paid special attention to the emigrants' diaries. Little by little, he had come to think of these people as old friends, and now he knew the nature and habits of each one; his favourites were young Jesse Applegate, the painter Alfred Jacob Miller, brave Narcissa Whitman, the dilettante Francis Parkman and his guide Henri Chatillon, old Ezra Meeker and the poet William Kelly.

When the girl came back from her walk she sat across the table from him and he looked at her face: hair black as coal, slightly slanted eyes of the same colour, prominent cheekbones that accentuated the thinness of her cheeks. He saw a fleeting shadow cross her thin, moving, beautiful face.

Shutting his book, he told the girl to go ahead if she had something to say. She began to talk about Wounded Knee.

"In December 1890," she said, "Sitting Bull has been assassinated and the Sioux have given up armed struggle. They are led to the edge of a stream called Wounded Knee, where they set up camp for the night. Soldiers surround the Indians to keep watch over them; they are men of the Seventh Cavalry Regiment. In the morning they decide to disarm the Indians. They have unlimbered four machine guns to suppress any resistance. Suddenly a brawl breaks out, and an Indian fires a shot. In a flash the soldiers unload their rifles on the Sioux warriors. Then the four machine guns send a shower of bullets into the women and children. There are a hundred and eighty dead in all. It is December 29, 1890. On New Year's Day 1891, grave diggers come to Wounded Knee and dig a mass grave for the bodies that are still lying on the snow; they find four babies who are still breathing, wrapped in their mothers' shawls. This is the end of the Indian wars. After the massacre at Wounded Knee, the Indians stop waging war against the United States Army. And that's it."

Darkness had swept into the municipal park.

Jack waited a few minutes; he wanted to be sure that she was finished and that the storm had passed. Then he lit a lamp and poured a cup of coffee, which he set on the table in front of the girl, with the sugar bowl and the pint of milk.

"Thank you," she said. "Is it late?"

"Not really," he said.

She sipped her coffee.

She still had something to tell, but it was very brief. She simply wanted to say that the Indians, too, had been guilty of massacres. And all that had started in 1849, when the discovery of gold in California had brought to the Oregon Trail hundreds of thousands of adventurers of all sorts who, unlike the first emigrants, had no respect for anyone or anything, who destroyed everything along their way and provoked the Indians' wrath.

XXIII

The Champion

Early July.

Jack was driving when they arrived at the Rockies. The great granite barrier, with its white and grey peaks, had been drawing nearer every day, and now came the climb. "Take your time," he said to the old Volks, which was struggling up the endless rises, and he frequently shifted into second gear and sometimes even into first in order to spare the small 1600 c.c. motor.

The man was getting worried.

"We have too many books," he said. "It's much too heavy on the hills. I shouldn't have brought my big dictionaries."

"Do you want to do like the emigrants?" asked the girl. "When they reached the Rockies they got rid of everything that was weighing down the wagons. Often they were things they were very fond of, but they had to throw them out, into the rocks and sagebrush. So the Oregon Trail was strewn with all sorts of objects, like oak furniture, grandfather clocks and musical instruments."

"It was ridiculous to bring the dictionaries," he said. "I haven't written a word since we left. Let's hope the motor holds out."

The girl was reading their favourite book. She said there was an incredible number of graves on this section of the trail. She didn't know if it was because of an epidemic or because the terrain was so uneven here, but there were graves all along the side of the trail. She would say: "Look, there's a grave right here . . . Look, here's another," and sometimes she would read the names: Mary Homsley, aged 28, Lucindy Rollins, 1849, Joel Hembree, aged 9, Ada Magill, aged 6, and a seventeen-year-old Indian woman whose name was Mini-Aku or Fallen Leaf.

Suddenly she cried out, ". . . lost . . . Platte River!"

Jack braked vigorously. The tires squealed on the asphalt, and the minibus skidded to a stop across the road. The box of groceries fell off the back seat, and overturned, and oranges rolled between the two seats. The black cat, who was sleeping in the kitchen sink, came and crouched on La Grande Sauterelle's lap.

The man parked the Volks beside the road.

"Are you crazy?" the girl exclaimed. "You could have killed us!"

"I'm sorry. You shouted . . . I thought we'd lost something. And quite frankly, it sounded as if we'd lost something in the Platte River!"

"It's my fault," she said. "I shouted because . . . with all those graves they talked about in my book, I was feeling lost, so I looked out at the river for reassurance: I like that river a lot and it was reassuring to see it every day . . . But it wasn't there! So I shouted, 'We've lost the Platte River!' That was ridiculous, I'm sorry."

"I liked it a lot, too," he said. "I'd even given it a nickname. I called it 'big two-hearted river' because of Hemingway's short story."

"That's a nice name."

"Thank you. Didn't the emigrants come to another river right away?"

"Yes, they walked for several hours and then they arrived at the Sweetwater River. They said the water was sweet . . ."

She coughed two or three times and continued, "You're very sweet, too. You could have got mad at me when I shouted like that for no reason, but you didn't: you're very sweet and gentle and patient and you never lose your temper."

"I've told you before: I'm not really gentle," he said sadly, kneeling to pick up the oranges; then he started the motor again.

He had a theory about gentle people. In his opinion, there was a distinction to be made between truly gentle and *phony* gentle people. The phony ones were weak or timid; life was hard for them and they were incapable of showing hostility. The truly gentle were those with self-confidence; they didn't feel threatened and felt no need for hostility. He placed himself in the first category.

"I don't care if your gentleness is real or phony, I still like you," said the girl as he drove back onto the road and picked up speed.

When they reached Casper, they left route 26. As the Oregon Trail turned southwest, they took the 220, which went in that direction. They had reached an altitude of fifteen hundred metres and the road was still climbing. Paying close attention to the sounds of the motor and the transmission, the man drove with the greatest caution: the muscles in his shoulders and the back of his neck were so tense that they ached.

A few kilometres past the town of Alcova, they arrived at the Sweetwater River.

They parked next to an enormous rock. Many emigrants had stopped there to carve their names and the dates of their passage on its rocky sides. Father DeSmet, a Jesuit, had called it "the Register of the Desert." La Grande Sauterelle had an idea: Jack thought it was totally ridiculous, but she wanted to go and see if Théo had left his name on the rock. She agreed that Théo had studied history and that no historian would commit such an act of vandalism; she agreed with everything Jack said, but she wanted to look all the same.

Jack was still protesting when, having left the Volks in the parking lot on the north shore, they were approaching the three-metre-high Stelco fence that blocked access to the rock; the National Park Service had put up the fence because "foolish and unscrupulous" tourists had written their names alongside those of the emigrants.

"Théo wouldn't have done that," said the man.

"Of course not," she said.

But they had already stuck their noses through the wire mesh and were trying to decipher the names and dates that were half obliterated by time.

Most of the inscriptions were later than 1850. The names were those of adventurers who had gone to California in search of gold. They also found inscriptions from the 1840s, among which they recognized, with pounding hearts, some of the men and women they had got to know from reading excerpts from their diaries, whom they had come to consider almost as friends and travelling companions.

They walked slowly along the fence. When they reached the other end the girl had to acknowledge that Théo's name was not there.

She thought for a moment.

"The Oregon Trail went along the south side," she said.

"Where are you going?" he asked, but she had already left; her stride was determined, and she wasn't even looking out for rattlesnakes.

The fence ended at the Sweetwater, and the river, though narrow here, formed enough of an obstacle to prevent visitors from getting to the south side. Undaunted, the girl climbed the fence and circled the rock. The man did the same, but more slowly, watching where he stepped because their favourite book said: "Be most alert for rattlesnakes in the weeds at the base of the rock."

She had already peered at a good portion of the south face when he caught up with her.

"Come look!" she exclaimed.

From the south side, the rock resembled the shell of an enormous turtle. La Grande Sauterelle was perched on the highest part, and far above his head the man could make out vultures soaring in the sky. But he couldn't see what she was pointing to at her feet.

"What is it?" he asked.

"Come here!" she exclaimed. "Otherwise you'll think I'm not telling the truth."

It was noon and it was hot. The man grumbled as he climbed the rock — truth, truth, what is the truth? — and when he reached the summit, he saw, between the girl's widespread feet, an inscription in red:

THÉO. 75

The truth was as red as a bloodstain.

As he did every time something important happened, Jack fell silent. He couldn't speak until they were back at the Volks, in the parking lot.

"It just says 75," he observed. "There's nothing to prove it was 1975. It could just as well have been 1875."

La Grande Sauterelle pointed out that the inscription had been painted on and that, in all likelihood, it couldn't be a hundred years old, but he would admit nothing.

"It could have been any Théodore or Théophile in 1875," he said.

"Why not Théophile Gautier?" she asked ironically. "I wonder if he was still alive in 1875. Just a minute . . ."

She looked up the poet among the proper names in the *Petit Robert*.

"He died in 1872," she said. "I was off by three years."

She took the wheel and, after starting the Volks, drove out of the parking lot and back onto route 220. Jack peered at the maps to see how far they were from Fort Hall: it was on the western slope of the Rockies and they still had a fair way to go.

The girl drove very well on hills. She didn't have to look at the speedometer to know when to change gears; she simply listened to the sound of the motor and she never made a mistake.

"Why not Theodore Roosevelt?" she asked.

"Huh?"

"Look in the *Petit Robert* . . ."

He muttered that the joke had gone on long enough, but nonetheless he looked in the dictionary: Teddy Roosevelt had lived from 1858 to 1919.

"You see?" said the girl. "And he made a number of trips out west. He had a ranch in Dakota or someplace like that. Before he was president of the United States he was a cowboy."

The girl's expression was impenetrable and, as usual, the man couldn't tell if she was being serious. They began to talk about cowboys. Jack told her that when he and Théo were little, a real cowboy was a man who pushed open the doors of a saloon and, by this simple act, caused a deathly silence to fall inside: the piano player would stop playing, the girls would climb upstairs, the poker players would become as motionless as statues, and the barman would dive behind the counter; but one man stood leaning against the counter, very tall and thin and dressed in black, drinking a beer as if nothing had happened, with his back to the man who had just walked in.

In the saloon, gripped by fear, everyone knew the story: some years earlier, the tall thin man in black had killed a man, and that man was the brother of the cowboy who had just entered the saloon.

In all those years, the cowboy had had but a single thought: to find his brother's murderer.

He had followed the trail from town to town, and now the hour of revenge had struck.

The two men would go out together into the dusty street flooded by sunlight; they would take fifty paces, then turn and stand motionless for a moment, facing each other, hands at their sides ....

....

Jack talked about his brother all afternoon. Of course he stopped now and then and talked about something else, but every time he said, "That reminds me . . ." or, "One day we were at . . ." and then he would tell another story.

It was not long before he realized that the tree houses fashioned from scraps of wood and spruce boughs, rafts made from old logs, vines tied to the stoutest branch for vaulting precipices or quicksand, or swamps teeming with crocodiles, playing cowboys, gangsters or tag volleyball, and even, when they played softball behind the church, the home run his brother had hit into the graveyard — all those exploits as well his brother's escapades at boarding school, the fact that he'd quit school to go to work, that he'd been the first to go out with a girl and that one day he had stuffed his belongings in a bag and left home to join the navy — he realized that they were not enough, so he added some more: he said that Théo had bought himself a Harley Davidson, that he could swim the St. Lawrence from Quebec City to Lévis, that he had spent two years with the Inuit at Povungnituk in the Far North, that he had driven Bruce McLaren's Ford GT40 in the trials at Le Mans 24-Hours . . . And little by little the outline of his brother grew and took its place in an imaginary gallery that included an odd collection of characters, among them Maurice Richard, Ernest Hemingway, Jim Clark, Louis Riel, Burt Lancaster, Kit Carson, La Vérendrye, Vincent Van Gogh, Davy Crockett . . .

WHEN NIGHT FELL, the cool mountain air swept into the old Volks, and all at once Jack felt a sense of sorrow against which he was powerless.

He picked up the cat and petted it for a long time.

The girl asked what was wrong.

"I'm a champion, too," he said with a woeful look. "I'm a champion at waking up in the middle of night and finding my old slippers with my toes and going to the kitchen in total darkness and making myself a hot chocolate WITHOUT EVEN TURNING ON THE STOVE LIGHT."

XXIV

The Great Divide

The road continued to climb. They were now at an altitude of 2,000 metres. However, the rise was gradual and the Volks was performing well.

One afternoon they arrived at a place called South Pass. It was neither a mountain pass nor a defile, as they had imagined, but a very broad plateau.

"Don't drive too fast," said La Grande Sauterelle.

The girl, who was very worked up, was consulting simultaneously the map of Wyoming she had pinned to the dashboard, their beloved book, which was in her left hand, and the big map of the United States, which was spread across her lap.

Suddenly, at the side of the road, they saw a billboard that read:

THIS IS THE CONTINENTAL DIVIDE —
EL. 7,550 FT. (2,302 M.)

Jack parked the Volks on the soft shoulder and they got out. The cat got out with them. They were standing on the very spot where the waters divided: ahead of them, the water flowed toward the Pacific, behind them, toward the Atlantic.

The girl looked in her book. The author said that, once the emigrants had come to the celebrated divide, they were eager to find a waterway, because they were curious to know what the water that flowed toward the Pacific Ocean would taste like; he remembered that the people who had come this way included not only all those who had emigrated to Oregon and California, but also a great many explorers and celebrated guides, notably Robert Stuart in 1812, Jed Smith, Jim Clyman, Jim Bridget, Tom Fitzpatrick and others in 1824, Captain Bonneville in 1832, Doctor Whitman and his group in 1835; and he deplored the fact that a place as important as the continental divide was brought to tourists' attention only by two modest blocks of stone that had been erected not by the government, but by "two private citizens at their own expense."

"We have to do something," said the girl.

"You're right. What can we do?" asked Jack.

"Something special. It's not every day that you cross the continental divide."

"What can two private citizens like us do that's special? Any ideas?"

"Yes. I'm starting to have an idea . . ."

Her voice was very odd and she had a sly expression.

"What's the most private thing that two private citizens like us can do?" she asked.

"Oh!" said the man. "Is that what you were thinking about?"

"Yes."

"Right now?"

"Why not?" said the girl, and took off her T-shirt: she was naked to the waist and she was about to unzip her jeans.

Jack looked all around.

"Do you see anybody?"

"N . . . no."

"So there's nobody around."

"Nobody."

"So do we do it or not?"

"You want to do it right now?"

"Yes!"

"Here?"

"YES! RIGHT HERE, RIGHT NOW, RIGHT ON THE CONTINENTAL DIVIDE!"

The cat scurried away and hid under the Volks.

The girl took off her jeans and her hunting knife, and then she noticed that the man still had all his clothes on. She helped him pull off his shirt, shoes and jeans, then she asked him if everything was all right and, without giving him time to reply, made him lie down on the shoulder of the road and started to kiss and caress him. He tried to say something, but she lay on top of him and kissed him harder, and just as he was trying again to free his mouth so he could say something, the girl felt under her belly a couple of shudders and a little flood.

"Oh, no!" she exclaimed.

"I'm sorry," he said, "but when I do it outside . . ."

"Yes?"

" . . . I get too excited and it happens too fast."

"Why didn't you tell me?"

"I didn't have time!"

"But you could have said anything — I don't know, you could have said: WATCH OUT! or STOP! or NO! That doesn't take long. Or you could have said HELP!"

"I'm sorry . . ."

"Or MAMA!"

"Why not MAN AT SEA!" he asked, and burst out laughing.

He had a good laugh, eyes half shut, but stopped when he realized that the girl couldn't shed her serious expression. He lay there on his back for a moment to see if she wanted to talk or do anything. The sky was deep blue above their heads and pale blue on the horizon where the mountains stood out against it.

The girl got up and dressed in silence.

She didn't say much for the rest of the afternoon. After the sun had gone down the air became cool, even cold, and Jack looked for a fully equipped campground so they could plug in their little radiator or their electric blanket. At Rock Springs they found a campground that was part of the KOA chain; it was more expensive, but they were sure of being comfortable and the girl would be able to relax and cheer up.

La Grande Sauterelle wasn't really in a bad mood; rather, she seemed preoccupied and a little sad. They spent the evening reading, each on his own side, and finally Jack got the bed ready and plugged in the electric blanket. It was a blue blanket, double-bed size, and they spread it over the sleeping bags when it was very cold.

Jack explained to the girl that the blanket's electrical system was divided into two independent parts: each part heated one half of the bed.

"The advantage," he said, "is that you can plug in half of the blanket if you're sleeping alone, or both halves if you're sleeping with another person."

"Are you saying that because you feel like sleeping alone?" she asked.

"Of course not . . ."

"Sure?"

"Absolutely. Now come on, or you'll catch cold."

La Grande Sauterelle got into the bed with him, and he plugged in both halves of the blanket. In a few minutes the cold and damp had given way to a gentle warmth, and for once Jack was soon asleep. He had been still for a good while when suddenly he realized there was something wrong with the girl; she was grumbling and sighing and tossing every two seconds. He asked her what was wrong.

"I'm not even a real Indian," she said.

"So?" he asked, still half asleep.

At once he regretted his words, because the girl burst out sobbing. He took her in his arms. He told her: "Don't cry, don't cry." He rocked her gently and stroked her hair.

"I'm sorry," he said. "I don't know why I said that."

"It doesn't matter."

She wiped her tears with the back of her hand. He rummaged under the pillow and found a Kleenex folded in four.

"It's clean," he said.

"I hope so!" she said, smiling through her tears.

Her smile vanished almost at once, though, and she began again to say that she was neither Indian nor white, but something in between and that, in the end, she was nothing at all.

The man didn't know what to say. He reached out to turn down the heat, because it was warmer in the bed now. The mechanism that controlled the temperature was in a small saucer-shaped case. The case was just above the bed, on the edge of the baggage compartment, and it served as a night light as well.

"I have something to tell you," he said.

He turned onto his side and drew up his knees.

"You say that you're 'something in between' . . . Well, I don't agree with you at all. I think you're something new, something that's beginning. You're something that has never been seen before. And that's it."

The girl heaved a long sigh and was silent for a moment.

"Thank you," she said at length. "Maybe I was a little *zouave*. Thank you very much."

A little later, they fell asleep in each other's arms and under the gentle warmth of the electric blanket. In the middle of the night the man woke up, and seeing the little light at the edge of the baggage compartment, he felt briefly as if a flying saucer was soaring silently above his head. It was absolutely idiotic . . . yet he fell asleep again and dreamed that La Grande Sauterelle was an extraterrestrial.

XXV

A Vagabond

Someone was hitchhiking. A man. White hair. A knapsack on his back . . . No, not a knapsack: a big piece of canvas, rolled up.

Jack looked at the girl to see if she agreed. She nodded, and he stopped the Volks level with the hitchhiker.

"Howdy!" said the old man.

"Howdy!" said La Grande Sauterelle.

She was trying to put on a western drawl. Her imitation wasn't very successful, because the old man asked, "You're from the East, aren't you?"

"Yes," she said.

"From Quebec," said Jack.

"*Je parle français*," said the old man, who had just a slight accent.

"You going far?" asked the girl, opening the door.

"To Oregon."

"We're going to Fort Hall," said Jack. "It's not very far, but you can come along if you want."

"Thanks a lot. It'll give my old pins a rest," said the man.

The sliding door opened only from the outside. Jack turned off the ignition and handed the keys to the girl. She stepped down, unlocked the door and opened it. The old man placed his canvas roll inside and gave the girl a rather comical salute before taking his place on the seat; he bowed, and bringing one leg back, he bent his knees slightly. She returned his bow in the same fashion.

"There's a cat in the sink," she warned him. "His name is Chop Suey."

"Cats are my friends," said the old man. "*Mes copains*, as you say in Quebec."

"Where did you learn French?" asked Jack.

"I lived in Paris. Between the wars, in 1921. Back then you could live in France fairly cheaply. Today, though . . ."

He didn't complete his sentence.

"And besides, on the road, I've met folks from Quebec . . . and often we'd travel *sur le pouce* together, as you folks say."

His French was accurate, but sometimes he hesitated in mid-sentence, as if he were mentally preparing the words he was going to use.

"Where did you live in Paris?" asked Jack.

"*Quartier Latin*," said the old man.

"What street, if you don't mind my asking?"

"Rue du Cardinal-Lemoine. If you want the number, I can tell you: I've got a very good memory!"

"Excuse me," said Jack.

The old man started to laugh.

Jack glanced in the rearview mirror: the old man was laughing openly; he had a fine face, plump and round, with deep wrinkles around his eyes, but the eyes were those of a crafty man.

La Grande Sauterelle turned toward the old man.

"Do you always hitchhike?" she asked.

He'd been doing so for a long time . . . But in his youth (an eternity ago), he hopped freight trains like many people at that time, because it was the Depression and there wasn't much money.

One way or another he'd been travelling all his life. He liked the road. It was his way of living. When he was tired he would lie down by the side of the road or in a field or park and cover himself with his canvas. Then next day he was back on the road again. There was an English word for that: the verb *to ramble*.

"In French, you can say *vagabonder*," said Jack.

"That's right," said the old man, without much conviction.

"Or *se promener, errer à l'aventure, aller de-ci de-là* . . ."

"Mmm-hmmm!" said the old man, and Jack didn't pursue the matter.

There was a moment's silence, then the girl started the conversation again.

"So you're going to Oregon?"

"That's right," said the old man, with a grin. "It's a fine place, one of the few where there are still plenty of wild spots by the ocean. I'm very fond of the Pacific, and I know a quiet place . . . There's a path you can't see from the road; it's hidden by vegetation, so you take that path, which is very narrow and . . . What's the French word for *steep*?"

"*Escarpé*," said Jack, and he couldn't resist adding: "*à pic* and *en pente raide*."

"Thanks. You go down that steep path, carefully so you don't kill yourself, and you come to a little cove where you find *nobody*, because *nobody* is exactly who knows about it."

That struck him as very funny and he laughed goodnaturedly.

"Nobody, that's me," he said. "I haven't got a house, but I do have a little cove hidden away somewhere in Oregon on the shore of the Pacific. At the back of my cove, there's a grotto I share with the crabs, and I have plenty of firewood. If you've got what you need for fishing, you can spend a week or two, but you have to bring something to drink. If you've got something to drink, wine or beer, and you catch some fish, it's heaven!"

They were driving toward Fort Hall, and the old man was petting the black cat, who had climbed on his knees. He was telling them all sorts of things because he was glad to have someone to talk to.

When he was heading out west, to the little cove that only he knew about, he always took the Oregon Trail: it was the oldest trail in America. It was older than the history of the conquest of the West, older than the *coureurs de bois* and the pioneers, older than all the emigrants with their ox-drawn carts. It was as old as the Indians and probably as old as America.

"When you travel out west," he said, "you feel best when you're on the old Oregon Trail."

"Will you stay in Oregon very long?" asked the girl.

"No. Just till fall. Then I go down to California and in the spring, I head back east."

"So you travel west," said Jack, "and when you get there you come back east?"

"I know," the old man laughed. "Sometimes I think it's ridiculous, too. Do you know the song 'No Roots in Rambling'? It's by Jerry Jeff Walker."

"No," said Jack.

"I know it," said La Grande Sauterelle.

She began to hum the melody, and the old man accompanied her, crooning some of the words now and then. It was a very sweet, nostalgic country ballad, and Jack managed to catch a few phrases such as: "I'm now alone and I know I need to ramble" and "It's the call from deep inside" and "The blues will haunt me till I die."

When the old man and the girl stopped singing all that could be heard was the Volkswagen's engine and the tires hissing on the pavement. They had left the Sweetwater River and route 220. They had crossed the Idaho border. They were travelling now along route 30 and driving through a town called Soda Springs, after the mineral springs the emigrants had found there. La Grande Sauterelle announced that they were just ninety kilometres from Fort Hall.

And the questions started again.

The girl asked the old man where he liked to spend the winter when he was on the Atlantic coast.

"Key West," he replied without hesitation.

Jack looked at him again in the rearview mirror.

The old man continued. "I've been to Cuba a few times, but I like Key West a lot. It's a good place to spend the winter. You're going to ask me why. Well, there's several reasons: the boats, the old houses and the cats. And the climate, of course."

He said that Key West never got very cold in winter. The nights were sometimes a bit chilly — *frisquet*? — but as soon as the sun rose, it would start to warm up. Some fishermen he knew would let him sleep on the deck of their boats or give him a meal in return for a hand with hauling in the nets, cleaning the kitchen or any other sort of job that could be done quickly.

The old man didn't like to work for too long. What he'd rather do, in Key West, was walk through the streets, lanes and little alleys in the centre of town and admire the old frame houses. With their big galleries trimmed with gingerbread the houses of Key West made him think of old ladies in lace gowns. They were wrapped in greenery and surrounded by gardens where stray cats would come to take shelter in the rich and secret shade. If he was unhappy the old man had only to stroll through the town and look at the old houses, and that would cheer him up.

La Grande Sauterelle wasn't often a mother hen, and she hated herself when she was, but this time she couldn't help it.

"You've never had a house?" she asked in an odd voice.

"Of course, like everybody else," said the old man.

"Whereabouts?"

"Not far from here, in Idaho. A village by the name of Ketchum."

At these words Jack slowed down in spite of himself, and the girl looked to see if there was anything wrong on the road, but everything was normal.

"It's near Sun Valley," said the old man. "You know the place with the famous ski resort?"

The girl pricked up her ears for a moment and listened to the engine, but it was turning over fine.

"Now and then I get an urge to see the house again," he said. "When I nip over there, to Ketchum, I sit in the restaurant across from the house and have a coffee. Sitting by the window, you get a good view of the house. You can even see people going out the side door to the garden."

The old man added that the owner of the restaurant was a friend of his and that he made very good coffee.

Then he was silent.

Neither La Grande Sauterelle nor Jack dared to ask the identity of the people who went out the side door into the garden.

"He makes very good coffee," the old man repeated softly.

Then he was silent until Fort Hall.

As they were turning off route 30 to the campground, the old man asked them to stop.

"I'll get out here," he said, standing up.

"You aren't coming to the campground?" asked the girl.

"Costs too much."

The girl looked at Jack and decided. "Be our guest!"

"Well, if you insist . . . !" said the old man, laughing.

"We insist," said Jack.

About six o'clock, Jack was making spaghetti and meat sauce while La Grande Sauterelle was at the swimming pool. The old man was off by himself; he was sitting at the foot of a tree reading *The Valley of the Moon* by Jack London, his favourite author.

The girl came back. When she saw that Jack had made enough spaghetti for three, she suggested they invite the old man.

"I'll go and get him," she said.

She draped a big beach towel over her head and shoulders and went to find the old man. He accepted with pleasure but insisted on bringing his "modest contribution."

Jack set the table, then took a can opener and opened the old man's "contribution": a can containing half a dozen little sausages.

"Oh!" he said. "Sausages!"

"German sausages," said the old man.

"Ah!"

"Cooked in beer."

"Oh!"

The German sausages cooked in beer weren't exactly the sort of thing Jack liked at suppertime, with his delicate stomach, but he was glad to see them, anyway, for he had imagined the can filled with a good three or four dozen sardines swimming in oil.

He couldn't stand sardines.

"Do you think I could add the sausages to the spaghetti sauce?" he asked La Grande Sauterelle.

"I haven't the faintest idea," she said, "but why not?"

He sliced the sausages and heated them in the sauce for a few minutes. When the meal was ready, they all agreed that German sausages cooked in beer improved the taste of spaghetti considerably. Then they talked about Théo, and the old man declared that he couldn't say if he'd run into him along the road.

"What do you mean!" Jack exclaimed. "If you'd met him you'd certainly remember him."

"Six feet tall, two hundred pounds — that's not uncommon out west," explained the old man.

"Yes, but he . . . he speaks French, he has curly black hair . . ."

"I'm awfully sorry," said the old man, "but I'm not sure. Maybe yes and maybe no."

He had met lots of people on the roads and trains. One night he'd even met Jack Kerouac. It was in a train somewhere around Denver, and Kerouac wasn't yet a famous writer. It was cold.

They had drunk wine. He remembered Kerouac very well, but he couldn't say about Théo.

Jack tried to be as objective as possible. He calmly told the old man everything he'd learned about his brother since the start of his journey. He gave all the details he knew, omitting nothing and adding nothing. He ended his account with the Oregon-California option, then fell silent. He let the old man talk. The account had been hard on him and he was glad it was over.

"If I was in your place I wouldn't hesitate," said the old man.

"Oh, no?" he said.

"No."

"What would you do?"

"Go to California. Your brother isn't the type you run into in Oregon."

"It's big, California."

"He'd be in San Francisco at this time of year."

"Why?"

The old man shrugged.

"Just like that," he said.

"But you," said Jack, "you're going to Oregon . . ."

"I'm a rambler, even a tramp, you might say," he said, "but I'm not a bum."

After they had eaten, the old man helped with the dishes, then went off to sit and read; he read Jack London as long as there was enough light.

"Weird," said the girl.

"He thinks he's Hemingway," said Jack. "Did you notice?"

"No."

"He says he lived in Paris, on rue du Cardinal-Lemoine . . . He talks about Cuba and Key West, and he says he used to have a house in Ketchum, Idaho . . . It's Hemingway's life!"

"I didn't know."

Jack shook his head.

"It doesn't make any sense."

"Maybe," she said, "but it's no worse than the rest. We've travelled two-thirds of the way across America, following a trail that's so slight . . . so slight and so incredible that if we told people nobody'd believe us. They'd think we were crazy."

"A real pair of *zouaves*!"

"And then to top it all off we pick up an old hitchhiker and he tells us there's a good chance Théo went to California, not Oregon! He's never laid eyes on your brother, but he says without the slightest hesitation that he went to California."

"San Francisco, to be precise! He even knows which city!"

"We should have asked for the address . . . Maybe he'd have given it to us!"

"And a letter of reference!" said Jack.

He began to laugh.

"And the worst thing is," he said, serious again, "the worst is that if this keeps up, the two *zouaves* will probably go to California . . . What do you think?"

"It seems to me the two *zouaves* don't really have much choice," replied the girl.

The sky was cloudy. The old man slept under the picnic table, wrapped in his canvas. When they woke up next morning he had already gone.

XXVI

The California Trail

At Fort Hall, they took a secondary road going southwest; this road, which would bring them to Interstate 80 in Nevada, was the Gold Route, the California Trail.

La Grande Sauterelle was driving slowly because of the road mice. These little animals — somewhere between a field mouse and a squirrel in size — stood on their hind paws by the side of the road, watching the vehicle pull up, then at the last moment they would cross. You had to constantly jerk the wheel or slam on the brakes to avoid them. The girl's nerves were shot.

The altitude had decreased. The landscape was now very arid. On either side of the road were greyish expanses of ground spotted green by sagebrush.

Jack was concerned about the road mice, too, but he was even more concerned about the old Volks. In midafternoon, when the heat was most intense, what he had been afraid of finally happened: the engine began to cough.

He tried to sound reassuring: "Grit in the gas tank," he said.

The engine coughed again, then stalled. The girl barely had time to pull the minibus over to the shoulder. She tried to start the motor again, but in vain.

"I'll have a look," said Jack.

He got out and opened the motor compartment. He shrank back because of the heat it gave off, then stuck his head inside and glanced briefly at the various parts of the motor.

"Try again!" he shouted to the girl.

She tried the ignition: the engine turned over but it wouldn't start.

"What's going on?" she called.

"I haven't the foggiest!"

Then she got out. The man was peering into the engine compartment, and she asked him what he was doing.

"Looking at the battery," he said.

"Don't do that!" she said. "If the starter's working, the battery . . ."

"Oh, you're right."

"It must be the gas: sounds like it isn't getting to the carburetor."

"Could we be out?"

"When we left Fort Hall we had three-quarters of a tank," said the girl.

There could be a leak in the gas tank, but the man didn't bring up that possibility. Instead, he checked the oil. Without a word he pulled out the dipstick, wiped it between his left thumb and forefinger like the old mechanics, put it back in and withdrew it again to examine the level of the oil.

"It's fine," he concluded, his tone as detached as possible.

The girl turned her head to one side, listening intently in the spot where the gas pump was.

As unobtrusively as he could, Jack slipped his oil-stained fingers in the left-hand pocket of his jeans; he hoped he would find an old Kleenex there, but his fingers encountered nothing, and he had no choice but to wipe them on the white lining of the pocket.

"Listen!" said the girl. "Do you hear something?"

"No — oh, now I do! A kind of whistling."

"Like a teakettle when the water's starting to boil?"

"Exactly."

"Crap!" she said. "It's a vapour lock."

She listened a second time.

The man awaited her explanation.

"When I was trying to avoid the road mice," she said, "I pushed the engine a little too hard and it heated up, so some of the gas vapourized; the sound you hear now is the vapour whistling inside."

She pointed to the gas pump.

"The vapour fills the pump and prevents the gas from getting to the carburetor," she said.

"What can we do?"

"I'm not sure. What would you do if you were by yourself?"

"Me?" he asked. "I'd stand by the road, on the soft shoulder, and I'd flag someone down to help me and then . . ."

"And then?"

"Then a truck would stop a — big ten-ton Mack — and out of it would step a tall girl with hair as black as a stove and legs as long and thin as a grasshopper's and she'd come and take a look at the motor and then we'd make an important decision."

"What's that?"

"We'd decide not to do anything. We'd find a little spot in the shade and we'd have a beer or we'd, well, we'd do certain very pleasant things, taking our time, and meanwhile the engine would cool down and the problem . . ."

". . . would solve itself," she said. "That's not a bad idea, but . . ."

"But?"

"There's another possibility: if the gas isn't getting through, it could also be because the filter on the gas pump is clogged."

"We have to clean the filter?" he asked, wiping his brow.

They weren't even moving, yet they were both soaked in sweat just from standing in the sun.

"That's the best thing to do," she said. "It'll give the engine time to cool down. We'll be taking care of two things at once and we'll be sure we've done them right."

"Have you ever cleaned a gas pump filter before?"

"Go get my tools," she said by way of reply, then added, "please."

The man went to get the tool kit from behind the passenger seat. The girl took out a vise grip and slid under the Volkswagen; she pinched off the rubber pipe that went from the tank to the engine to block the gas intake. She explained to Jack what she had just done. Then she unfastened the gas line which led to the pump and began to take apart the pump itself.

She worked methodically, explaining everything she did, and the man tried to anticipate her needs and to place the tools that she would need within reach.

As she was working in the sun, he made a sort of awning for her with the flannel blanket. So she wouldn't have to remain crouching, he brought the little yellow vinyl stool from the Volks. He had poured some cold water into a big dish, and from time to time he wiped her brow with a damp towel.

It took the girl about half an hour to take the pump apart; to prepare for reversing the procedure, she arranged all the pieces in the right order on a newspaper beside her. After she had cleaned the filter, which was very dirty (she showed it to Jack with a certain satisfaction), she spent twenty minutes reassembling the pump and putting everything back in place.

As the work proceeded, the man found it harder and harder to conceal his admiration and to contain his enthusiasm. And when everything was done and the engine turned over like new after a few times, he gave free rein to his feelings. He told the girl, whose face was smeared with grease and whose hands and arms were black to the elbow, "You're the most beautiful mechanic I've ever seen! I adore you!"

Then he indulged in all sorts of linguistic excesses. He declared, for example, that mechanics was the science of the future; that it was more important than literature and philosophy.

And so forth.

The girl smiled and said nothing. Finally the man took the towel and a big bar of Sunlight soap and washed her face, then her hands and arms. Both of them were smiling blissfully.

XXVII

Old French Songs

They were travelling through Nevada, along Interstate 80, and they had been listening to the radio for some time.

It was very hot inside the Volkswagen, even with the windows open; one western song followed another, melting into the silver-grey colour of the asphalt that stretched endlessly before them.

It was a slow day. They had been listening to country music for two hours: Johnny Cash, Woody Guthrie, Jerry Jeff Walker, Kris Kristofferson, Jack Elliott, Roy Acuff and other singers they didn't know. La Grande Sauterelle, who was at the wheel, turned the knob in search of another station, and she came across a program devoted entirely to old Jimmie Rodgers songs. So they listened to "Train Whistle Blues" and the other old western songs to the end. When the program was over, Jack wanted to hear the news; he turned the dial from one end of the AM band to the other, then he tried all the FM stations, but he found only country songs.

He switched off the radio.

"Know what?" he asked.

"What?" said La Grande Sauterelle.

"I'm in the mood for an old French song."

A gentle smile formed on the girl's lips.

The man repeated, "I miss the old French songs."

"Do you?" she asked.

"Yes, I do. It just hit me."

"And — did you have any particular song in mind?"

He didn't reply immediately. He yawned and stretched like a cat. He had a number of songs in mind, and he was taking his time. He was in no hurry at all to make his selection. It was pleasant to let the old songs turn around in his head for a moment. They spun like records, and each one was performed by the singer he liked best for that particular song.

Finally he made his decision:

"The one I miss particularly is '*Le Temps des cerises*,' sung by Yves Montand."

"Yves Montand sings it very well," the girl admitted. "Nana Mouskouri does it pretty well, too, but good old Yves Montand is hard to beat."

"I think so, too," said the man, grinning.

"And what if La Grande Sauterelle were to sing it?" asked the girl.

"I'd be curious to hear that," he said.

She pretended to be turning on the radio and, mimicking the sprightly style of a variety show host, she announced that station CKRL-FM, 89.1 on the dial, was pleased to present a song dedicated to all those travellers on the endless roads to the west who were fed up with country music.

She cleared her throat and began.

Quand nous chanterons le temps des cerises
Et gais rossignols et merles moqueurs
Seront tous en fê-ê-te

Her voice wasn't full and rich like Yves Montand's, needless to say, nor was it sweet and melodious like Nana Mouskouri's; it was a throaty voice, somewhat dry and husky. But she sang in tune and just fluidly enough to follow the melody very closely as it rose and fell. And it became jolly, rather bawdy even, when she came to the words:

Les belles auront la folie en tête
Et les amoureux du soleil au coeur

Then it grew more tender and melancholy for the second verse, which began:

Mais il est bien court, le temps des cerises . . .

La Grande Sauterelle didn't remember all the words, and now and then she filled in with "la-la-la." She had forgotten most of the last verse, and the only words she still remembered were the following:

C'est de ce temps-là que je garde au coeur
Une plaie ouverte
Et dame fortune . . . ne pourra jamais
Fermer ma douleur.

XXVIII

An Expedition for Someone to Talk To

"We're going to stop at a ranch," said the girl.

They had crossed a desert region; for two days they had seen nothing but gloomy, grey expanses that made them think of lunar landscapes.

And they hadn't talked to anyone except campground and service-station attendants. "How are you today?" and "Have a nice day!": those were the only words they had exchanged with the local population during those long days.

That was why, as soon as there was greenery to be seen again, they decided to "go looking for someone to talk to." It was La Grande Sauterelle's idea. More precisely, she wanted to make an expedition to a ranch.

"All right," said Jack, who was driving. "It may be our last chance before California. I've never been on a ranch."

"Me neither," she said. "Maybe they'll invite us to have

something to eat and then we'll go for a horseback ride!"

"Apparently Westerners are very hospitable. I read that in the literature on Nevada."

"So did I."

They had also read something about the large ranches found in the northern part of the state. It even said there were Basque shepherds and flocks of sheep. They looked over the fields all around them, but they saw nothing. No cows or horses or sheep.

"There aren't even any houses by the roadside," said Jack. "It's as if we're still in the desert."

"Maybe the houses are set back, far from the road," said the girl. "Know what I think?"

"What?"

"I think we should turn onto the first private road we see. I'm sure that any private road will take us straight to a rancher's house."

"We can try," said the man, his voice betraying a certain apprehension.

They drove another twenty kilometres before they spotted a dirt road that started at the Interstate and disappeared far away toward the north. There was a fence, but it was open and there was also a sign that read:

NO TRESPASSING

"It sounds like a bad translation of *trépasser*," said Jack. "Forbidden to depart this life," he snickered, steering the old Volks onto the private road. "We'll tell them we're looking for a shortcut to Carson City. That's Kit Carson's town."

"They're bound to believe us," said the girl. "Especially because the road goes north and Carson City's to the south . . ."

"Sorry."

"It doesn't matter," she laughed. "We'll think of something."

"Sure."

They weren't going to let some insignificant details stand in their way. Nothing could diminish their pleasure at the prospect of being entertained on a Nevada ranch.

The ranchers would say: "Quebec in Canada? Oh, long way from home!" And then they'd invite them inside, where it was cooler, for a drink. And they'd say that their neighbour had a son who was working in Canada. "*Ah, oui*? Is that so? Whereabouts, if you don't mind my asking?" "Calgary, he's in the oil business!" "Very interesting, but Calgary's in the West, you know, whereas Quebec . . ." "Is that so?" And they had another neighbour who had a daughter working in Halifax? Well, it's true Halifax is in the East, but you know, Quebec actually isn't that far east: it's somewhere between the two. See what I mean? Get the picture?

And Jack would nudge the girl with his elbow to tell her it wasn't polite to say "get the picture" to their hosts, but the ranchers would be broad-minded and wouldn't take offence at a small breach of etiquette. They would invite the visitors from Quebec to take a horseback ride around the ranch and give the cowboys a hand as they rounded up the cattle in the corral, if they weren't too tired. Then they'd invite the visitors to eat with them, because *as a matter of fact* they had prepared a huge barbecue that very night. All their neighbours within a hundred-kilometre radius were coming over to eat and celebrate with them.

Jack and La Grande Sauterelle were having a lively conversation about the size of the T-bones they were going to eat at the giant barbecue when suddenly they saw the rancher's house at the end of the road.

It was a large two-storey frame house with a very wide veranda on which, from a distance, they could see chairs and a table.

They didn't see any people.

They saw trees, a swing under the trees, an old tire hanging on a rope from a branch, but no children.

Absolutely nobody.

Jack stopped the Volks in front of the steps that went up to the front door.

He opened the car door . . .

As his foot touched the ground a police dog pounced on him. He had just enough time to get back in the minibus.

Immediately two other police dogs emerged from under the veranda and hurled themselves at the Volks, barking furiously. The three huge dogs, drooling, lips curled, fangs threatening, ran around the old Volks, leaping up at the windows. One of them — the one that had appeared first — lunged at Jack. He put his front paws on the windowframe, stuck his head inside and clamped his jaws shut, just missing the man's left arm; his teeth snapped on the air because Jack had instinctively flung himself to the right.

The man and the girl rolled up the two windows, closed the air vents and locked the doors.

The dogs were German shepherds. They were tan and black. They kept circling the Volks and barking, and from time to time they jumped up, trying to attack the passengers.

The black cat, hiding under a seat, gave a muffled growl.

Jack started the engine and drove slowly away from the rancher's house. The three dogs accompanied the Volkswagen for several minutes, then wheeled together as if someone had called them. Jack looked in the rearview mirror, but he didn't see anyone at the house. They drove along in silence for a while.

Then the girl asked, "Want me to drive?"

"It's okay," he said. "Thanks."

At the end of the dirt road they got back on Interstate 80 and the black cat came out of its hiding place.

"Our expedition wasn't a success!" said the man.

"We'll try again another time," said the girl calmly.

"It's true, not all people are dogs," he said.

The girl gave him an odd look.

He realized his slip and corrected himself: "I meant, not all people have dogs."

XXIX

The Ghosts of San Francisco

"It's made half of steel and half of dreams," said Jack.

"It's the most beautiful one I've ever seen in my life," said the girl.

"When I was little I thought it was made of gold. I was sure it had been built with the gold that was discovered in California."

They were talking about the Golden Gate Bridge, which they had spotted in the distance on the right, emerging from a mass of fog, as they turned onto the Bay Bridge to cross the bay that separated them from San Francisco.

The journey was nearing its end.

They had set out from Gaspé, where Jacques Cartier had discovered Canada, and they had followed the St. Lawrence River and the Great Lakes, then the old Mississippi, Father of Waters, to St. Louis, where they had taken the Oregon Trail and, following the trail of the nineteenth-century emigrants who had formed caravans of ox-drawn wagons to set out in search of the Lost Paradise, they had covered the vast prairies, crossed the continental divide and the Rocky Mountains, forded rivers and traversed the desert and still more mountains, and now they were pulling in to San Francisco.

The city was blanketed in fog.

The man and the girl didn't know where to go. As they drove off the bridge they took a street that ran along the wharves; the street, which was called the Embarcadero, led them to various tourist attractions: Fisherman's Wharf, the Cannery (an old brick building that had been turned into boutiques and stores), a small beach, an old fort, a maritime museum, a yacht club, a park called Victoria Square and finally the Palace of Fine Arts, vestige of the 1915 World's Fair.

They strolled along the wharves and in the shops, but there were really too many tourists . . . and people trying to sell things to tourists; they quickly found both groups unbearable and took refuge on the little beach.

They sat in the sand.

The island of Alcatraz was across from them. And when they turned around to look at the city they could see cable cars clattering down the steep slope of Hyde Street with their load of tourists, the strange clang-clang of their bells sounding at every intersection. On the hillside, the pastel tones of the houses softened the landscape.

The girl took off her running shoes and went to the shore of the bay. She stood motionless for a moment, her feet in the water, eyes fixed on the beige walls of the old Alcatraz prison. Then she turned toward the man, who was sitting in the sand with the cat on his knees, and saw that he, too, was looking toward the island.

"It's late summer but the water's as cold as on the North Shore!" she said. "What are you thinking about?"

"Burt Lancaster," he said.

"Because of *Birdman of Alcatraz*?"

"Of course. And because he's one of the actors my brother Théo liked a lot, too. My brother also liked John Wayne, Gary Cooper, Alan Ladd, Randolph Scott, Kirk Douglas . . . And what about you — what were you thinking about?"

"Indians. They took over the prison in 1969 and declared the island Indian territory."

She was smiling.

"And what happened?" asked the man.

"The police set up a blockade around the island," she said, "and then . . ."

She spread her arms in a sign of impotence and, swivelling on her bare feet, turned toward the city and bowed deeply. Her gesture seemed to say that the Indians always lost, that they had lost here yet again and there was nothing to be done about it. It was fate or something of the sort.

"All the same," she said, "It's a beautiful city!"

"Yes, but it's cold!" said the man. "Shall we go?"

The sun couldn't break through the fog, and they were shivering because of the dampness that sliced through to their bones.

They were eager to get back to the Volkswagen. The man took the wheel. After glancing at a map of the city, he decided to drive along Bay Street for a while, but he turned right and took Columbus when he saw a sign indicating that North Beach was in that direction. The name North Beach evoked memories of the beatniks and Jack Kerouac.

On the Road was one of the books La Grande Sauterelle had "borrowed" during their journey because it was mentioned in the police file in Toronto. She had found a French translation of it in a Kansas City bookstore; she knew it already, but she had enjoyed reading it again. "If you haven't reread you haven't read," she would say. As for the man, he had preferred to keep intact the memory of his first reading: he recalled a journey that seemed like a continual party, described in a powerful style that was as tangled as the vast roads of America; he had merely reread the preface, where he had underlined this sentence:

> The road has replaced the ancient trail of the pioneers heading West; it is the mystical link that joins the American to his continent, to his compatriots.

They saw at once that North Beach was a very special neighbourhood, so they left the old Volks in a Safeway parking lot at the corner of Chestnut, pulled on sweaters and set off down Columbus Avenue. Even though the black cat had grown since the start of their journey, he still allowed himself to be carried in La Grande Sauterelle's hood: instead of sleeping curled up in a ball in the hood, now he stood up, his chin and front paws resting on the girl's shoulders.

They passed a red brick building that housed a neighbourhood library. A little farther, on the left, was a park called Washington Square.

"Ah, yes," said the man, "Kerouac used to come here often."

He talked as if Jack Kerouac were an old acquaintance; in fact, he had read only two of his books and a few magazine articles about him.

"Once, he had bought a gallon of white wine," he said. "His favourite wine at the time was a cheap brand of Tokay. So he went into the park with his jug of Tokay and he started drinking. He sat at the foot of a tree and drank until there wasn't a drop left, then he was completely drunk and he fell asleep in the grass."

Washington Square was an ordinary park, a square of green with trees, benches, a few statues and a corner for children, but all at once, with Kerouac's presence, everything was transformed. Suspicious forms lay in the grass. The grass must have been wet from the fog, yet old men and bums lay there asleep, wrapped in newspapers or canvas. The park was filled with ghosts of the past.

La Grande Sauterelle reflected.

"We should have stopped at the library," she said.

She was right: perhaps Théo belonged to the library. They retraced their steps and pushed the door of the brick building.

The librarian was a tall thin girl with long black hair. She bore a strange resemblance to La Grande Sauterelle, except that her features were half-Chinese and half-Mexican; because of her dual parentage, her face was gentle, somewhat strange and very moving.

Théo's name did not appear on the list of members. La Grande Sauterelle asked the girl if she could look at the lists for previous years, too. The girl shook her head: the old records were in the central library in the Civic Center, on Van Ness Street. She looked at them with great patience and a warm smile. Jack told her briefly about his brother, and she gestured that she understood. She said that if Théo had stayed in North Beach, one man who could give them information about him was the owner of the Café Trieste. She wrote down the address on a piece of paper. It wasn't far. They could walk.

"Thank you very much!" said Jack, shaking her hand. "That's very kind!"

"You're very welcome!" she said, and her slanted eyes twinkled.

La Grande Sauterelle leaned across the counter, put her long thin arms around the girl's neck and kissed her on both cheeks.

"That's exactly what I wanted to do," said the man once they were outside, "but I never dare to because it embarrasses me and I'm afraid people will think I'm a dirty old man."

Outside, the fog had lifted. It was eleven o'clock in the morning. The sun was magnificent and the street was flooded with light. This time as they passed Washington Square, where ghosts of the past lingered, they noticed the enormous phallus of the Coit Tower, which stood at the peak of Telegraph Hill.

They were walking along Columbus, looking all around them. They encountered all sorts of people — Chinese, Italian, French, German — and the air was filled with the aromas of coffee, pizza and pastries. A hill rose on their right and another on their left, and both were covered with blue, pink, white or yellow houses with projecting windows; they found themselves in a sort of little valley.

At the corner of Columbus and Vallejo, the girl stopped, blocking traffic; passersby were obliged to walk around them.

"What is it?" asked Jack.

"Nothing special," she said, "just that I feel good. It's been a long time since I've felt so good."

The cat climbed up on her shoulder. She took him in her arms and tried out a dance step on the sidewalk. All at once she stood still.

"Look!"

She was pointing to a sign on Vallejo Street, on their left: the Café Trieste.

"I'm hungry," she said. "What time is it?"

"Almost noon."

They walked into the Trieste. The café was crammed, but they found a little table in a corner. There was no table service. Jack went to order sandwiches and coffee at the counter: it was a good opportunity to talk to the owner, but he didn't dare.

"What did you say to him?" asked the girl when he came back with their lunch.

"I said, 'Two sandwiches and two cappuccini.'"

"And then?"

"Then he said, 'Small or big, the cappuccini?'"

"And then?"

"Then I said, 'Small,' and that's all."

"Can you imagine!" she said, laughing. "He travels all the way across America and he can't ask, 'Do you know a guy named Théo?'"

"I should have brought a picture," said Jack. "I don't understand how I could forget such a thing."

"I'll go and talk to him," said the girl, taking a sip of her coffee.

She handed him the cat and headed for the counter.

Jack was expecting to see the owner shake his head, but instead he smiled. He seemed to be explaining something. Near the door, across from the counter, some people sitting on the windowsill were having an animated conversation. Other people were alone. A girl was reading the classified ads in the *Bay Guardian*. A thin man with Spanish features, very black hair and a dark complexion held a guitar on his knees, but he wasn't playing. The wall on Jack's left was covered with pictures, some of which had been taken at the Trieste.

La Grande Sauterelle came back with the owner. He took her to the wall and showed her a photograph of a group of people sitting around a table; he put his finger on one of the figures in the picture.

"That's him," he said.

"Thank you," said the girl, and the owner went back to his counter.

XXX

Mr. Ferlinghetti

They crossed Columbus Avenue, and Jack was still in an emotional state when they entered the City Lights Bookstore. He repeated, "When he said: 'That's him . . .'"

"I know," said the girl.

"I thought that . . . It gave me a shock!"

"I understand. I'm sorry."

The man whom the owner of the Trieste had pointed out in the picture was not Jack's brother. It was Mr. Ferlinghetti. Lawrence Ferlinghetti, the poet.

The owner didn't remember Théo, but he had told La Grande Sauterelle she should go and see Mr. Ferlinghetti because he knew all the important people who had lived in North Beach. In the photograph, Mr. Ferlinghetti looked like a man about fifty, with a grey-and-white beard, thick eyebrows and an aquiline nose; he was wearing a white shirt open over a T-shirt and a dark vest on top of the shirt; he looked pleasant and distinguished. He was the owner of the City Lights Bookstore. The girl had asked permission to borrow the photograph, and the owner had replied that it was very dear to him because it had been taken at the Trieste; however, it was reproduced in a book they would certainly find if they went to the bookstore: the title of the book was *Beat Angels*.

There was a young man in charge of the bookstore. They learned from him that the owner wasn't there just now, but that he came almost every day. He might turn up at any moment or late that afternoon or the next day. Or the day after that.

City Lights was a wonderful bookstore. Jack liked bookstores very much and one of the finest he had ever seen was called Le Bouquiniste; it had been located on a little street, Desjardins, in Quebec City, when he was a student — it didn't exist anymore. The most wonderful of all, of course, was Shakespeare and Company. During a visit to Paris, Jack had remembered that Hemingway mentioned it in *A Moveable Feast*. He had gone to the address indicated, on rue de l'Odéon, but the bookstore was no longer there; it had moved. He had hunted for a long time and one fine day, as he was strolling along the quays, he suddenly noticed the famous black-and-gold sign. He liked that bookstore because it had been a meeting place for writers he held in high esteem — Hemingway, Scott Fitzgerald, James Joyce, Gertrude Stein and others — but also because there were books everywhere, and little aisles and all sorts of nooks and crannies and even a narrow staircase up to the second floor from which, on the day in question, had come the gentle air of a guitar.

At City Lights — the bookstore at North Beach, in San Francisco — the staircase led to the basement. Downstairs and up there were quantities of magazines and periodicals, in addition to the books; the poetry section was especially rich, and there were a table and chairs for people to sit and lounge.

La Grande Sauterelle was sitting downstairs reading an anarchist publication when Jack came down the old wooden stairs four at a time. He was very excited. He laid a book before her on the table and began to leaf through it, muttering something. She saw that it was *Beat Angels*.

"Look!" he said.

She recognized the picture she had seen on the wall of the Café Trieste.

"It's the same picture," she said, not understanding why he was so worked up.

"I know, I know, I know," he said. "But did you see the man sitting in the middle?"

He pointed to the centre of the picture, to a man with a beard and very black curly hair.

"I didn't notice the first time," he said, "but . . ."

"Are you telling me that . . . ?"

"Yes, yes, it's my brother! Isn't that incredible!"

"Are you sure?"

Beat Angels, Edited by Arthur and Kit Knight, p. 11.

Lawrence Ferlinghetti, Minette Le Blanc, Peter Le Blanc, unidentified man, Allen Ginsberg, Harold Norse, Jack Hirschman and Bob Kaufman, Café Trieste, Grant Avenue and Vallejo, San Francisco, 1977. Photo by Diana Church.

"Absolutely!"

The girl began to get excited, too. "This is amazing!"

She got up, walked around the table, then sat down again.

"He's sitting at the same table as Mr. Ferlinghetti," she said. "That must mean that the owner knows him!"

"I suppose so," said Jack.

"And this picture isn't very old: it was taken in 1977! This is fantastic."

Arm in arm, they climbed the stairs and crossed the two rooms on the ground floor to see if Mr. Ferlinghetti was there, but he hadn't come in. They waited another hour and then, as their excitement had dropped, they were feeling tired. They realized it would be better to come back later. The girl "borrowed" the book and they left. They took a room at the San Remo, a small hotel near the place where they had left the Volkswagen.

In their room, which was even smaller than the ones at the YMCAs, the man kept looking at the picture of his brother.

"One thing bothers me," he said, "that's the caption under the picture. They name everybody, but when they get to my brother all they can say is 'unidentified man.' 'A man without an identity.' It's a little like sayng 'a man without importance,' isn't it?"

"Not at all," said the girl. "It just shows that the photographer — who was the photographer, anyway?"

"Her name's Diana Church."

"It means she didn't know your brother, that's all. The morning she developed the picture she didn't feel too well; she was feeling a bit rocky because she'd had too much to drink the night before, probably with the people in the picture, and she didn't have the slightest desire to do any research, so she just wrote 'unidentified man.'"

"People have no professional standards anymore," said Jack severely.

"What's the world coming to!" the girl added.

The man laid the open book on the bedside table and stepped

back several paces.

"There's something else that bothers me," he said. "When I stand back and look at the picture, it's ridiculous but it makes me think of Leonardo's painting *The Last Supper*. And my brother . . ."

La Grande Sauterelle drew up and looked over his shoulder. He went on:

"With his big head of black curly hair, I can't help thinking my brother looks like Judas."

"That's ridiculous," said the girl. "Ridiculous and even morbid."

"I know," he said, "but I can't help thinking it."

WHEN THEY EMERGED from the San Remo about four in the afternoon, the fog had come back and the city was grey and cold once more. They walked along Columbus Avenue to the bookstore. The owner still wasn't there, and they roamed around the neighbourhood.

City Lights Bookstore was at the corner of Broadway, in the nightclubs and sex shops area. Huge pink posters offered all the wonders of eroticism and sensual pleasure. The nightclubs had names like Naked City, Casbah, Chi Chi Club, Condor, Garden of Eden. At the door of each establishment a man urged people in, telling them they'd have a good time and that everything was free.

They walked up and down Broadway, then strolled in neighbouring Chinatown. They rested for a while in a park called Portsmouth Square. An old woman feeding pigeons told them that the bench on which they had taken a seat was the one where Robert Louis Stevenson used to come to sit and write. Before she walked away into the fog, she added that it might have been on this bench that he had written *Treasure Island*. Once again they felt surrounded by ghosts of the past.

They were walking south. Following Powell Street they walked to Union Square and a little beyond. This was downtown: an odd mixture of business people, artists and bums. At the corner of

Powell and Market there were many bizarre characters. People who seemed lost. They weren't too badly dressed and they weren't really poor, but their eyes shone with a strange light; they talked to themselves and seemed not to know exactly where they were, who they were and what they were doing there.

Just before five o'clock, they went back to City Lights. The owner wasn't in.

He didn't come the next day, either.

On the afternoon of the following day, as Jack and the girl were leaving the bookstore and preparing to go back up Columbus Avenue, they spotted Mr. Ferlinghetti, a briefcase under his arm, coming in the opposite direction. His manner was very distinguished, but he was wearing blue canvas shoes like the Chinese. He seemed a little tired.

He paused without looking at them and entered the bookstore.

Jack and La Grande Sauterelle turned. As they were about to enter, however, Jack grew hesitant; he lingered outside, reading the titles of the books in the window: there was *Howl and Other Poems* by Allen Ginsberg and *The Electric Kool-Aid Acid Test* by Tom Wolfe and also *Clean Asshole Poems* by Peter Orlovsky . . . and then the girl gave him a firm push in the back.

Mr. Ferlinghetti was behind the counter, talking with the young man. Jack took a copy of *Beat Angels* from the shelf, opened it to the page with the photograph, but couldn't make up his mind whether to question the owner. The girl asked him what was going on.

"This feels too much like playing detective," he said.

"What do you mean?" she asked.

"I feel like a character in a B-movie. An old one with Jean Gabin or Humphrey Bogart. You know the type: there's a sleazy smoke-filled bar with ceiling fans, and the detective comes up to the counter and shows the bartender a photo. 'Have you ever seen this man?' The bartender says he's never seen him in his life, so then the detective puts a twenty-dollar bill on the counter:

'Maybe this'll refresh your memory.' And the other man says, 'Right, now I remember . . .' See what I mean?"

"Of course," said the girl, smiling.

Just then the owner approached them.

"*Soyez les benvenus*," he said. "Are you French?"

"Not exactly. We're Québécois," said Jack, who was glad to see that Mr. Ferlinghetti spoke French.

"Been in San Francisco long?" asked the owner.

"Just two days," said Jack. "We're looking for someone . . ."

He thrust the photograph under Mr. Ferlinghetti's eyes.

"Do you know this man?" he asked.

"Sorry?" said the owner.

"This one here," said Jack, putting his finger on the picture of his brother.

Mr. Ferlinghetti peered attentively at the picture.

"I remember the occasion," he said a few moments later. "It was at the Café Trieste in . . . that's right, it's written there . . . in 1977. I remember very well, but this man . . ."

"He's my brother," said Jack.

"What's his name?"

"Théo. I've been looking everywhere for him. I haven't seen him for a long time and . . . he's my brother," he said again.

The owner of the bookstore looked pensively at Jack, then studied the picture again. He was rummaging in his memories. Searching.

"I remember him," he said at length.

La Grande Sauterelle's face lit up with a smile so broad and luminous that for a moment Mr. Ferlinghetti was distracted from what he was about to say; he turned his head toward her and looked at her in silence.

"Yes, I remember," he resumed. "He had a very . . . pronounced Québécois accent. He came to the poetry readings and he was often at the Café Trieste and the Vesuvio. I think he was staying in North Beach . . . or he had a girlfriend in the neighbourhood. I don't remember which exactly. It's been a few years now . . . A lot of people have gone or disappeared, you know."

He stopped to reflect.

"I haven't seen him in . . . five, six years."

"It doesn't matter," said Jack. "Thanks a lot."

"I'm sure we'll find him," said La Grande Sauterelle.

"I don't know if he's still in North Beach," he said, "but you could put an ad in the Bay Guardian, with the picture."

"That's a thought," she said. "You're very kind."

"Wait . . ."

He touched his brow with his forefinger.

"I thought of something," he said. "The girl who was with him still lives in North Beach. She works around here. Come, I'll show you."

He followed them outside and went up Columbus Avenue with them as far as Broadway, where he stopped. He pointed to the sign outside a nightclub across the street, on the other side of Columbus.

"You see the Condor?" he asked. "Then Tony's restaurant?"

"Yes," said Jack.

"Then the big red-and-white sign on the left?"

"Yes."

"That's where she works," he said. "Her name's Lisa. *Bonne chance!*"

He shook hands with them, then turned and walked away. They gazed at the big red-and-white sign that read:

HAVE A PRIVATE TALK WITH
A LIVE NAKED GIRL. ONLY $1.

XXXI

The Girl in the Showcase

Eight p.m.

The door to the nightclub was open, but there was a red velvet curtain. Moving the curtain aside, they could see, just inside a big room, a man who was probably the manager: he was sitting behind a counter. The room was divided into two sections: on the right were cubicles in which you could watch films and on the left, a series of glass showcases.

"How are you tonight?" asked the manager.

"Fine, thank you," said Jack.

He put two dollars on the counter.

"We'd like to see Lisa."

"Sure."

The manager pressed a button.

"Go to the last showcase."

"Beg your pardon?"

"*La dernière vitrine*," he repeated in French.

"Oh! Thank you."

"Have a good time."

"Thank you very much."

They went to the back of the room.

The last showcase was lit by the bluish light from a bulb that hung from the ceiling. There was nothing in it but a wooden stool.

A moment later, a door opened at the back of the showcase and a naked girl stepped out. She was smoking a cigarette. She sat on the stool and absently scratched her thigh.

Jack called softly, "Lisa?"

"Yes?" she said.

Curls of blue smoke drifted around the girl and rose lazily to the light bulb. There was a round opening in the glass at face level to facilitate communication with clients.

"Do you speak French?" asked Jack, leaning toward the opening.

"*Bien sûr que je parle français*," said the girl.

She had a slight east-end Montreal accent.

"My real name's Lisette," she said.

"I'm Jack. And this is La Grande Sauterelle ... I'm looking for a man called Théo. I understand that you know him and I'd like to know where I can find him."

"Who told you that?"

"Mr. Ferlinghetti."

The naked girl looked more attentively at Jack. She looked him up and down and then she examined La Grande Sauterelle in the same way. It was obvious that she suspected them of being from the police or perhaps the RCMP. She asked them to step back and turn around slowly.

"There's something weird in your hood," she told La Grande Sauterelle.

"It's a cat. He's asleep."

"Let's see . . ."

La Grande Sauterelle turned around, and Jack picked up the cat so the girl in the showcase could see it.

"That's okay," she said.

The girl was reassured. Her face was beautiful, expressive and intelligent and very pale, with dark eyes. She asked about Quebec. She wanted to know if independence would be coming soon. She had been born near Parc Lafontaine in Montreal. She had travelled a lot. She'd been to India and to South America.

Jack showed her the picture of Théo.

"You want to know where he is?" asked the girl.

"Yes," he said. "I've looked for him everywhere. He's my brother."

"Your brother? There is a resemblance, but he's taller than you, and heavier."

"That's because he takes after my father. I'm more like my mother."

She bent down to put out her cigarette on the concrete floor of the showcase.

"I can't say *exactly* where he is."

"No?"

"He left North Beach. Things have changed a lot around here. It's not like it used to be."

"You haven't seen him since?"

"I saw him once."

Jack approached the showcase.

"Where?"

"Listen," said the girl, "life's hard on everybody. Some people can't stick it out and it's rough . . . They let themselves drift along on the current and they go under . . ."

La Grande Sauterelle broke in, "You mean they pass through Chinatown and wash up around Market Street?"

"Yes," said the naked girl.

"And that's where you saw him last?"

"Yes."

"Around Market and Powell?"

"Right."

Jack gathered his courage to ask, "How was he?"

"Not in good shape," said the girl sadly, and stood up to let them know that she didn't feel like talking anymore and that the conversation WITH A LIVE NAKED GIRL was over.

She left in silence through the back door.

The blue light went out.

XXXII

Théo

They moved out of the San Remo Hotel and into the Stratford, on Powell Street.

It wasn't a luxurious hotel; it wasn't the St. Francis or the Fairmont or the Hyatt Regency, but they had a big room with two large windows that looked out on the street. And they were just a minute away from Powell and Market.

The intersection of those two streets formed a very lively square with a cable car terminal, busy bus stops, a subway station, numerous stores and restaurants, newspaper stands, itinerant salesmen, florists, musicians and all sorts of passersby and idlers, among whom from time to time Jack and the girl spotted those bizarre individuals they had noticed before: vacant-eyed people who talked to themselves and wandered around like ghosts.

At the entrance to the subway station there was a sort of little open-air amphitheatre made up of galleries where public benches and ornamental plants had been set out. These galleries were below street level, sheltered from the wind that blew in off the Pacific. In all of downtown there was no better place to warm yourself in the sun.

Usually Jack and the girl ate their meals in a cafeteria on Geary Street. Sometimes, though, they would go to the Burger King at the foot of Powell Street; they would have a very economical meal: if they had a "bacon double cheeseburger" at noon, they didn't need a snack at four o'clock and didn't feel hungry before seven or eight at night.

They strolled through the neighbourhood, and the days passed.

One day, to get their minds off things, they took the Volks and went to the Haight-Ashbury district where the hippie movement had flourished during the sixties. They didn't expect to meet any hippies, but they hoped to see traces of the movement, some reminders that thousands of young and not so young people from every part of the country had come there to try to put into practice new ideas about life and human relations. All they saw were boutiques and restaurants. Jack declared that storekeepers were the most stable people in the world.

"They can survive all changes and fashions," he said. "One day there'll be nobody on earth but storekeepers."

In the city centre, Jack and La Grande Sauterelle had struck up a friendship with an old woman who supported herself by playing electric guitar and singing. She would set herself up on the east side of Powell Street (the side that got the afternoon sun), across from Woolworth's, on a folding chair, and she would sing old songs like "The Kentucky Waltz" by Billy Monroe.

The woman's voice was strong and deep, though a little hoarse, and as her guitar was plugged into a loudspeaker she could be heard from a fair distance, and many people would stop for a moment and toss coins in her guitar case. Jack and the girl would sit on the sidewalk and listen to her. Between songs, she told them what it had been like in the past, in the East, when she was part of a group of musicians. She said that she sang now to warm the hearts of the men and women who had once had a house, relatives and friends somewhere in the vast land of America and who, after losing everything, had drifted along on the current and washed up on the shores of the Pacific.

They liked the woman, because of her songs and because of the things she told them, but they liked her for another reason, too. One day the man had shown her the photograph of his brother, and she said that she saw him now and then. But she wasn't sure it was him because his hair was grey, not black.

One afternoon, when La Grande Sauterelle was walking through some neighbouring streets, Jack was sitting on the curb and talking with the old woman. She was reminiscing about the past again. She was saying that old Billy Monroe was her hero.

"Don't talk to me about heroes!" said the man.

"Why?" she asked.

"I've travelled a long way and all my heroes . . ."

He didn't complete his sentence because La Grande Sauterelle came running up. The cat was clinging to her shoulder and his ears were flattened back.

"He's there!" she exclaimed.

"Who?" asked Jack.

"Théo!" she said. "He's there, I just saw him."

She pointed to the corner of Powell and Market. She was out of breath.

Jack got up, very excited.

"What? You saw him? Where? Are you sure? How long ago? Did you talk to him?"

When she had got her breath back, La Grande Sauterelle replied that she had just seen him. She hadn't talked to him, she'd come at once. He was in the sort of amphitheatre across from the subway station. In the tier in the middle. Sitting on a bench.

"What's going on?" asked the old woman, but no one answered her.

"All right, I'm going right now," said Jack.

He ran off, then stopped and came back.

"Will you wait here for me?" he asked the girl.

"Of course," she said.

She kissed his cheek and gave him a friendly little push. He took two or three steps — and came back again. He gave her the keys to the hotel room.

"You might need them," he said.

"Thanks."

Then he spoke to the old woman. "Excuse me, I have to go and see somebody over there."

"That's all right," said the old lady.

"He's my brother."

"Sure," she said, smiling. "He's your brother."

La Grande Sauterelle gave him another little push.

"You're always pushing me," he said, and this time he left for good.

He ran along the sidewalk, then crossed the street, just missing a cable car, went around a florist's display and, cutting his way through the mob of people at the corner of Powell and Market, he came to the subway station. He leaned over the brass railing that went around the amphitheatre.

The tier in the middle? No, he wasn't there.

There were people on all the benches, but he didn't see Théo. He looked everywhere.

Suddenly he saw him: he had grey hair, and he looked like an old man, but it was him!

It was Théo!

He was sitting on a bench with some other people in the middle tier, and he was warming himself in the sun. He was sheltered from the wind. His hair was really very grey. Almost white. With eyes half shut against the sun, he was looking at what was going on down below.

And down below, in the centre of the open space opposite the subway station, there were circus trappings: a number of wooden crates, unicycles, Indian clubs, torches, top hats, musical instruments. In big letters on one of the crates were the words:

LOCOMOTION VAUDEVILLE

The people coming out of the subway were sitting on the steps or the ground. Jack waved at his brother, but Théo wasn't looking in his direction. Anyway, there were more and more people, not just down below but also in the middle tier and up above, around the brass railing.

Now there was no more room down below.

It was better to stay up above.

He mustn't lose sight of Théo.

A clown had just arrived. He wore no makeup but 'Bounce the Clown' was printed on his T-shirt. He was a short man, ageless or perhaps in his forties; he was bald, with a few lank wisps of hair on either side of his head. He was spinning a ball on his finger. He mingled with the spectators and talked with them. When he saw a child he would ask it to raise a finger in the air, and spinning the ball a little faster, he would balance it on the child's finger.

Two other performers had arrived, a man and a woman, and they were juggling with the Indian clubs. The woman, who was very thin, wore a multicoloured costume; she was smiling. The man looked serious and wore black.

Théo was serious, too. He sat there motionless, his face imperturbable. Jack was watching the performers, but he was also keeping an eye on his brother. He felt a hand on his elbow: It was La Grande Sauterelle.

"I got too nervous to wait," she said.

"I'm glad you came," he said, making room for her along the railing. "I didn't dare go down: there's too many people, and I was afraid I'd lose sight of him. I was afraid he'd go away. It'll be easier with the two of us."

They worked out a strategy. When the show was over the girl would go down the stairs while Jack stayed up above to warn her in case Théo suddenly decided to go and take the subway; once she was on the middle tier she would take over the surveillance and Jack would join her.

Outside the subway station down below, the performer dressed in black was now perched on a unicycle that stood more than two metres high. Over his black sweater the other two had placed a straitjacket and given him twenty seconds to get out of it. The spectators were shouting, "Twenty! . . . Nineteen! . . . Eighteen!" and the performer went into contortions to free his arms, while struggling to keep his balance on the unicycle. When he had only five seconds left he unfastened the straps as if by miracle, tossed it over his head and jumped down to salute the applauding crowd.

The show was over.

It was cold and damp because the fog had come back. as it did late every afternoon.

"I'd better go down right away," said the girl.

But she stood rooted to the spot.

Jack, too, was stupefied.

Something strange was happening in the middle tier. The men sitting on either side of Théo . . . they had got up, they had taken hold of something behind the bench. It was a wheelchair.

All at once the two men placed Théo in the wheelchair. They leaned over and lifted Théo so they could climb the stairs. Then one of them pushed the chair toward a van parked a little farther away alongside Market Street.

"Let's go!" cried the girl.

She started to run along the sidewalk, zigzagging through the passersby. She had almost reached the van and was talking with the two men when Jack caught up with her. A retractable ramp had been taken out of the vehicle, and one of the men was about to push the wheelchair inside.

"One moment, please," said the girl.

She took both men by the arm and they grudgingly consented to move away a few steps with her.

Jack positioned himself in front of the wheelchair.

His brother didn't raise his head, so he crouched in front of him so as to be in his line of sight.

"Théo?" he said softly.

His brother's eyes were staring at him and there was a sort of silent question in his gaze, but the rest of his face was devoid of expression.

He touched his hand.

Théo showed no reaction. His hair was grey and his beard was more white than grey. He wore a track suit, jogging shoes and a heavy black turtleneck sweater; the collar was really very thick.

He raised his voice. "It's Jack! It's your brother!"

Théo's eyes squinted as if he were making an effort to understand. His cheeks were hollow, and there were creases on either side of his mouth and bags under his eyes. There were tufts of grey hair in his nose and ears. He moved his lips and saliva dribbled from the corner of his mouth.

Jack took a Kleenex from the pocket of his jeans and wiped the saliva. Then he grabbed Théo by the arm and shook him, crying, "THÉO IT'S ME! IT'S YOUR BROTHER!"

When they heard the cries the two men rushed up and one of them set about reassuring Théo.

"It's all right," he said several times, then pushed the wheelchair inside the van. The other man pointed out to Jack that disabled people were very sensitive and that one should speak softly to them, especially when dealing with paralysis. Jack said he was sorry. He asked the man to tell him whatever he knew about this paralysis, beginning with the exact name of the disease. The man replied that he was a volunteer and that he wasn't competent to answer the question; his colleague, though, was a social worker.

Before replying, the social worker took care to shut the sliding door of the van. He began by saying that there was a medical file for every patient at the agency and that information could be obtained from the doctor. As everyone could see, the name and address of the agency, which specialized in helping the handicapped, appeared on the sliding door of the van. Then he made an effort to recall the precise name of the disease. "They call it creeping paralysis," he said finally.

"Creeping?" Jack repeated.

The man nodded.

Jack looked at La Grande Sauterelle. In the girl's worried gaze he saw the same image that the word *creeping* had suggested to him: a man crawling along the earth like an insect.

He didn't have the strength to protest when the social worker pointed out that it was time for him and his colleague to return to the agency with their passenger.

XXXIII

La Grande Sauterelle

That morning, for once, the sun was shining over San Francisco Bay. As they drove along route 101 toward the airport, the girl said that she remembered how the sun had been shining over the Baie de Gaspé on the day in May when they met.

"I remember," said Jack. "It was a beautiful day."

"Yes, I was on my way to Gaspé to see my mother . . ."

They were early and the girl was driving slowly.

"That day," she said, "I didn't expect to be going to San Francisco."

"Neither did I," said the man.

"I'll take care of the Volks, I promise."

She was very glad that Jack had decided to leave her the Volkswagen. She was going to check out of the hotel and live in the minibus because she didn't have much money. She wanted to spend a while in San Francisco: she thought that city, where the races seemed to live in harmony, was a good place to try to come to terms with her own twofold heritage, to become reconciled with herself.

"Anyway, weren't you born in a mobile home or something like that?" asked Jack.

"A trailer," she said.

The man looked at his watch, but it was an automatic gesture: he had at least an hour and a half before his plane took off for Montreal.

"And of course you're a mechanic . . . The Volks is better off with you than with me. It's so old."

"One of these days, perhaps I'll bring it back to you," she said.

"It's done more than two hundred thousand kilometres," said the man.

"Yes, but it's still tough."

"You don't have to bring it back."

"I know."

They had talked about it already. They had talked about the Volks and about everything that mattered two days earlier, when they came back from the agency that looked after disabled people. The doctor had told them that Théo's paralysis was progressive and that no one could do anything. His memory had been affected and he didn't really know who he was, but with the competent and attentive care being lavished on him, he was not unhappy; in fact, he was as happy as a person could be under the circumstances. Trying to bring back the past might aggravate his condition.

Jack took the black cat in his arms.

"You're still thinking about Théo?" asked the girl.

" I . . . the idea that it's better not to see my brother again . . . I accepted it so quickly that . . . now I wonder if I really loved Théo. Perhaps I only loved the image I'd made up." He shrugged and said half seriously, "One of these days I'm going to have to learn something about human relations."

"*You* could write about it in a book," she suggested in the same tone.

"What do you mean?"

"You've said that writing's a form of exploration, haven't you?"

"Did I say that?"

"Yes. At the border. Between Windsor and Detroit."

La Grande Sauterelle suddenly slowed down and turned left off the 101, onto the airport road.

"There's a remark by Daniel Boone I like a lot," she said, driving the minibus toward a parking lot. "I don't remember where I read it, but he said, 'Sometimes I feel like a leaf in a whirlwind. It may spin and swirl and turn but it keeps moving ahead.'"

Jack said nothing. When she had parked the Volks and turned off the ignition, he told the girl he would rather go into the airport by himself.

"There's going to be a big empty space in the Volkswagen," she said.

The man petted the top of the cat's head, then behind his ears and under his chin.

"You'll probably meet someone," he said.

"Generally I'd rather be alone."

"Me too."

He turned toward her. "But we spent the whole summer together."

"You can't always be logical!" she said.

Then they hugged each other, sitting on the edge of their seat, knees tangled, and sat there motionless for a long moment, embracing tightly as if they were a single person. After that Jack took the little suitcase he had packed and left the Volks, and the girl started the engine. When he turned around to wave, she said, "May the gods protect you!"

He waved until the Volks had disappeared, and when he walked into the airport alone, he was smiling in spite of everything at the thought that somewhere in the vastness of America, there was a secret place where the gods of the Indians and the other gods were meeting together in order to watch over him and light his way.